Shweta Bachchan-Nanda is a columnist for *DNA* and *Vogue*. A well-known personality, she is the daughter of actors Jaya and Amitabh Bachchan. Shweta is married to Nikhil Nanda and is the mother of two children. She has her own clothing label, MxS, which launched in 2018. She lives in New Delhi. This is her first novel.

SHWETA BACHCHAN-NANDA

Paradise Towers

HarperCollins *Publishers* India

First published in India by
HarperCollins *Publishers* in 2018
A-75, Sector 57, Noida, Uttar Pradesh 201301, India
www.harpercollins.co.in

2 4 6 8 10 9 7 5 3 1

P-ISBN: 978-93-5302-315-7
E-ISBN: 978-93-5302-316-4

This is a work of fiction and all characters and incidents described
in this book are the product of the author's imagination. Any resemblance to actual persons, living or dead, is entirely coincidental.

Shweta Bachchan-Nanda asserts the moral right
to be identified as the author of this work.

Typeset in 11.5/16.2 Sabon LT Std at
Manipal Digital Systems, Manipal

Printed and bound at
Thomson Press (India) Ltd

MIX
Paper
FSC FSC® C010615

This book is produced from independently certified FSC® paper to
ensure responsible forest management.

To my grandfathers, Dr Harivanshrai Bachchan and
Taroon Coomar Bhaduri,
for their gift of words

In a leafy Mumbai suburb, on the very turn of a U bend, stood the handsome structure of Paradise Towers, a residential building, built in the late sixties, as the last word in modern convenience. By 'modern' the builders meant that it had an elevator with a designated liftman, and a garden that most bungalows would be envious of, with its designated gardener.

Over the years, other, more modern and loftier structures came up in the area, dwarfing Paradise Towers. However, none could compete with its clean lines, meticulous planning – which kept it from flooding during the rains – or its residents.

The building stood a few metres from the beach, and depending on the time of day, it enjoyed either a balmy breeze or the stench of drying fish. The road it stood on was more a by lane that rarely saw any traffic besides the random vegetable vendor and fisher women, who with baskets on their heads, crossed over to their fishing village via the building twice a day.

The facade of the building was vanilla white and got a new coat of paint every five years. On it was painted in bold, brick-red letters: Paradise Towers, vertically, with the 's' in 'Towers' dangling just above a balcony on the first floor. That was another one of its unique features, whereas the buildings around Paradise Towers were painted steel grey, their windows tinted black, Paradise Towers boasted a substantial balcony for every road-facing flat. It was a building law that the occupants were not allowed to hang their drying on the balcony, so as the years went on, it retained its aesthetic appeal while the places around it got cluttered and messy.

The entrance was a wrought iron gate with arrowhead bars secured by a sickle lock mechanism. A smaller pedestrian gate was attached to it, and was most often used by visitors and residents alike.

A metal-sheeted guards' cabin stood outside the gate, though its inhabitant preferred to sit outside it, on a folding chair, his register and desk fan jostling for space on a rickety stool in front of him.

A wide concrete driveway led to the ground floor where, in a maze of pillars that defined parking spots, stood the elevator. A staircase, right by the lift, wound its way up the building, every even numbered set of stairs being followed by a landing.

The elevator was placed so that it divided every floor in two, with a flat on each side and a small lobby in front of it. The staircase also allowed access to each floor and the substantial terrace, accessible to all and used for the drying of clothes, housing of water tanks and the electrical room, and where all the staff gathered to moan about salaries and to gossip.

Rarely, in the spring, the building children would go up there to fly kites, but as the years wore on, and more modern modes of play were invented, the children lost interest.

The flats were spacious and airy, with large windows that let in the sunlight. They each had a small kitchen, staff quarter adjacent to it, and two bathrooms.

The garden downstairs was lush and lined with bougainvillea creepers on the boundary wall, which spilled onto the road, shedding petals and carpeting the street pink. Well-tended flowerbeds with seasonal flowers ran all over the circumference of the garden, breaking only at its entrance, and a mud path ran alongside for those who wanted to walk. Palm trees flanked the driveway on one side and there were talks of installing a water fountain, which was then scrapped in favour of leaving the driveway with a roundabout used for potted plants and a seating spot for the maids to keep an eye on their wards, who often played in the garden.

The residents of Paradise Towers were an amenable bunch. They all interacted with each other, and their children were constantly in and out of one another's flats. The women had a committee, which organized Diwali and Christmas parties yearly, and once even a seventieth birthday party. There were fast friends and sworn enemies, but seldom any grave unpleasantness.

Nothing dramatic ever happened at Paradise Towers ... or so you might think. Of course, appearances can be very deceptive.

1

Mrs Kapoor gave the mouthpiece of her telephone a vigorous wipe with the end of her cotton dupatta and set it down with a sigh. Calls to her mother always carried on longer than she wanted. The phone had rung incessantly while she was taking the accounts from her staff, and she picked it up wondering why anyone would call on a landline if the matter was so urgent.

'Good morning, betaji,' came her mother's heavy voice from the other end when she finally answered it. 'Forgotten your Mummy? Big city, big life, no time for small town relations!' alleged the matriarch, rather unfairly, when indeed she had spoken to her daughter only last evening. As she had every single day since Mrs Kapoor had married and moved to Bombay.

'Sorry Mamma, I was taking the accounts,' Mrs Kapoor replied feeling terrible. Somewhere under the strained civility of her voice was the subtle jab of irritation. She was a good daughter, especially so after marriage, never wanting her mother, who lost no opportunity to remind her of the hardships of being a single mother, to feel forgotten.

'Haan haan bachche, of course you have a busy life. Not like me – a useless burden that you all have to endure. I don't know why god doesn't call me to him quickly,' spat back her mother, unconvincingly self-deprecating.

'Mamma, why do you talk like this? You know how much it upsets me. I was, in fact, just about to dial your number.'

'Achcha? Some khabar? I was just having my bed tea in the garden,' her mother said, suddenly cheerful.

'I wanted your gaajar halwa recipe, Mummy. I have been missing home and felt like making it for myself.'

'Of course. If you are missing home so much, beta, why don't you just call me to visit you. I'll make halwa for you every day … bade din ho gaye Mumbai aa kar,' she replied, ending her sentence with a wily laugh. The point was not lost on her daughter, who was used to her mother's taunts.

It had been a slow season for Mrs Kapoor's mother. Her friends and acquaintances were traveling, leaving her with little to discuss or poke her nose into. Suddenly she felt warmly for the daughter whom she had married and sent off so far away from her. Mrs Kapoor stuttered not knowing what to say. Just this morning her husband had told her: 'I sincerely hope you are not planning on calling your mother over. I have a lot of important meetings this month, our partners from America are in town and my boss expects me to look after them,' effectively dashing his wife's hopes of extending a much sought after invitation to her mother. She would never hear the end of this, thought Mrs Kapoor, and brought her mother's attention back to the gaajar halwa in an effort to change the topic.

After an agonizingly long conversation about the low-quality carrots one needed to settle for in Mumbai, she finally began reciting the recipe, which Mrs Kapoor scribbled down, tapping her pen on the pad every time her mother digressed, for which she was soon reprimanded: '…What is that tak-tak noise bachche? It is interrupting my thought flow. Either you do that or listen to me.'

'Haan ji, Mummy, I am listening.'

'Beta, I just remembered – yesterday I had gone to the market, aise hi, nothing else to do sitting at home…' She paused to drive that point home, 'At Gyanchand cloth emporium I picked up lovely material for a suit. First I thought I'll pick up extra for you, then I said chhaddo – where will she wear this? Mumbai is full of imported fabric. And, bachche, I kept it for myself only. Beautiful patterns these days in Bizzy Lizzy material.'

Mrs Kapoor, now running behind schedule by forty minutes, finally lost her patience and lied to her mother about hearing the doorbell ring and hung up. That was when the doorbell actually began trilling loudly all through the house, making her feel another wave of guilt. She called out to her houseboy Dinesh, instructing him to answer it in a shriller tone than she had intended.

૨๛

Dinesh, erstwhile house boy and man Friday to the Kapoor's for upwards of ten years, threw open the door only to find, instead of the milkman seeking payment, Lata, the liquid-eyed enchantress who worked for the Aly Khan family four floors down. Dinesh ran his hands through his hair, already unruly from a morning of housework, and gave her his most disarming smile. Lata, barely able to look him in the eye – his feelings for her were common knowledge in the building, making their encounters extremely awkward – nodded a hasty good morning, holding out a hot case tidily swaddled in thick white cotton. He received it carefully, avoiding contact with her hand. After all, he wasn't one of those

Lotharios who jumped at any opportunity. He would do nothing to make her uncomfortable.

'Gaajar ka halwa for your madam,' she breathed, her voice quivering. Slowly she raised her head to make eye contact, causing Dinesh's heart to lurch, then quickly turned around and hurried down the staircase. Dinesh lingered by the door listening to her rubber chappals clap against the marble stairs.

Four floors down, Lata let herself back into the Aly Khan flat.

༄

Mrs Aly Khan was the mother of five children, whose mornings always started early. Today, she was expected at her in-law's for lunch and the maulvi was taking longer than usual to finish tutoring her youngest two on the Quran. She checked herself in the mirror twice, then peeped out the door of her bedroom to find the threesome still at the dining table bent over a passage, and quickly shut herself in again. She could not risk catching the maulvi's eye for that would mean a further delay by half an hour and this she could not afford.

It was important to her that her in-laws approved of her. Her marriage to their eldest son was hard won. They were in favour of a match with the daughter of a second cousin, but their son had categorically refused and presented her to the family as his only choice. Ever since then, Mrs Aly Khan had taken it upon herself to win them over, an exercise that was both taxing and futile. She had been slaving over the stove all morning preparing her mother-in-law's favourite gaajar ka halwa. If there were ever to be a détente, her mother-in-law was her best bet: a kindly lady severely dominated by her husband's unmarried sisters. Mrs Aly Khan Jr had often felt that, given a chance, the elder Mrs Aly Khan would happily take the wife of her favourite child under her wing.

Spotting Lata, who had just entered the flat, she frantically gestured to her. Lata, on spying her mistress beckoning her through a half-opened door, quickly kicked off her rubber slippers and wiped the front of a foot on the back of her leg gingerly. Successfully avoiding any conversation, she walked past the maulvi and his pupils, their heads still bent industriously over their books, and discreetly entered the bedroom, closing the door behind her.

'Lata, did you give the halwa?' Mrs Aly Khan enquired while turning around so Lata could zip up her kameez. 'Yes, I gave it to Dinesh, madam.'

'Oh? Mrs Kapoor was not at home?' Mrs Aly Khan asked, her kameez zipped. She turned around and sat in front of her dressing table mirror fiddling with her hair while Lata put a starched, washed handkerchief into her mistress's handbag and carried it to her. 'I did not ask, madam,' the girl replied.

'How much longer for the children to finish? We are getting late. Please go out there and get him to wrap up. And then get the children to wash their hands before we leave the house,' Mrs Aly Khan instructed without moving her gaze from her reflection in the mirror. Lata nodded and walked out into the dining room.

Soon, the sound of chairs scraping against the floor signalled the end of class and Mrs Aly Khan waited to hear the front door click shut before she ventured out into the dining room.

Lata was rushing the scholars into their shoes when their mother stepped out with hair neatly braided and bag in hand, a vision. Mrs Aly Khan was slim as a reed even after five children, and had twinkling eyes that shone brighter when she was sad. Her hair reached her waist when left undone. It was no wonder, Lata thought, that her saab had gone against his family's wishes and married her. After talking to the cook, who had come out of the kitchen, pad and pen in hand awaiting instructions for dinner, Mrs Aly Khan plus two headed down to the parking lot and their waiting car.

2

The watchman drew open the gates as the Aly Khan Mercedes drove out, throwing dust onto his shoes. He gingerly wiped them on the leg of his khaki uniform trousers and went back to sitting on his weather-beaten bench, scribbling into his dog-eared and soggy register the time and number plate of the departing vehicle, as per building society policy. Looking up, he could see Mrs Mody on her balcony peering at him through her binoculars. Her thin, white claw-like hands, their nails painted a crimson red, grabbing onto the pair with an expertise born from years of poking her hooked nose into other people's business. She let down the binoculars, which dangle from the strap around her neck, and reached for a glass bowl on the table next to her before walking to an ornate white cage inside which sat a parrot, bobbing its neon green head and hopping from leg to leg as if needing to relieve itself. Mrs Mody opened the latch and placed the bowl inside. She then sat back as her beloved pet pecked away at its meagre meal, every now and then fluttering its feathers.

The oldest resident of this building, Mrs Mody and her late husband were the first occupants of Paradise Towers. It was they who hired the first watchman and kept a gardener to tend to the expansive garden and flowerbeds. They watched as slowly the flats were sold to various families and the community grew and flourished – the Kapoor's took the penthouse, the Aly Khans occupying the entire second floor to accommodate their brood. The first floor was Ranganekar's (whom Mrs Mody approved of the most on account of their seemingly spartan lifestyle – they hardly entertained and were prompt with society payments on building upkeep, alas despite her numerous efforts they were not one for much chit chat). She was on the third, and the fourth floor housed the Patel and Roy families, whose children got along like a house on fire though the parents were always simmering in disagreement over common areas – namely the stamp-sized space just outside the elevator. The fifth floor had two flats occupied in season, by two NRI Sindhi brothers and their families, whose names she would always forget.

The regular watchman being away at his village had sent his young nephew as temporary replacement, Mrs Mody took it upon herself to keep a sharp eye on him till such time as he was deemed trustworthy, so far he was passing muster. She untucked her Chantilly lace trimmed handkerchief from her watch strap and dabbed the sides of her mouth. She then confused the binoculars for her spectacles – also dangling on a chain from her neck – and pulled them up to her eyes so she could begin reading the day's papers, ironed and laid out for her by her man Friday, Patrick.

⁓

Mr Ranganekar scuttled from his path, on the way to his waiting Uber cab, to make room for the noisy arrival of a tempo followed shortly by a SUV bursting to the seams with people and boxes. His heart started to palpitate. What was this? He thought to himself. *New tenants?* He visualized the demise of his heretofore-peaceful existence by this car full of humans and it was more than his orderly mind could bear. He pulled himself upright and clipped on, hoping to avoid making pleasantries with the people who from the clicking of doors he knew would emerge from their overstuffed cocoon any second. The watchman fashioned him a salute and he nodded his head in a panicked greeting.

Meanwhile, behind him, the doors of the SUV flew open and started divesting itself of its curious cargo. Mrs Mody, on hearing the commotion, folded her newspaper and, after a brief struggle yet again between binoculars and spectacles, managed to find the appropriate viewing instrument and trained it on the intruders.

❧

The Singhs lately of Long Beach, New Jersey were a large family, even by Indian standards. Mr and Mrs Singh, second-generation Americans having met and fallen in love at a Target store during a pre-Christmas super sale (she on colliding with Mr Singh had dropped four tubs of her favourite Rocky Road ice cream all over his pants making a mess she was later thankful for, as it led to a rather unusual date at the laundromat where she promised to undo the damage and which ended with their first kiss), went on to produce four sons in the quest for a daughter, who eluded them. Mrs Singh had taken to dressing her youngest in girls' clothes and tying his hair in ribbons till he was two years old – if there was any lasting damage done to the young lad, it was yet to be ascertained. Having decided – after their third of four boys had been caught smoking pot and agitating to drop out of school to pursue a rap career – that perhaps the laxity of America was more than their boys could handle, they moved to repatriate the whole family in the hopes of sorting the boys out.

It was this musical progeny that was the first to tumble out of the SUV that morning, still plugged into his iPod, pants slung low on his hips. He stood there while boxes of various sizes and shapes were flung at him, which he caught and placed on the ground stacking them up to make a rather unwieldy tower. The automobile now empty of its inanimate objects, started clearing out the animated ones. Limbs appeared out of its many doors eventually lining up the entirety of the Singh family, eldest to youngest in descending order. The boys set to unloading the tempo while Mrs Singh looked around her new surroundings sizing it up, as indeed was Mrs Mody up on her perch sizing the Singhs up, for these were the new tenants that would occupy the empty first floor flat opposite the Ranganekars.

3

Mrs Roy, arms on hips stood staring down the elevator shaft, as if giving it one of her sternest looks would manage to restart the darned thing. The elevator was public property and Mrs Roy was furious that one family had managed to appropriate it for the bulk of the morning. So engrossing was this blatant disregard for common utilities that she had quite overlooked the appearance and hasty disappearance of her neighbour and sworn enemy Mr Patel. She stood there, draped in a crisp white cotton sari, her long wet hair patterning a damp patch on her blouse, intermittently stopping to interrogate passers-by on the status of the movers. Not satisfied with the smattering of intel coming her way, she wound her hair into a bun and, adjusting her pallu, set off to gather it first-hand.

The first floor was a chaos of cartons, discarded bits of masking tape and red and white stickers with the words FRAGILE printed on them in capitals. Baulking at the hysteria of it all, Mrs Roy drew the end of her pallu to cover her mouth and nose as if to prevent contagion, and peered into the Singhs' flat through the slight gap in the door when it opened to reveal a rather crumpled-looking boy whose clothes seemed to be patched together with pins and slogans! Her eyes widening, she muffled a hasty greeting that was reciprocated with an upwards jerk of the head as the boy meandered around her to salvage another box from the landing. Mrs Roy shook her head in disapproval of this blatant flouting of building protocol and punched the doorbell with her pinky finger while the others kept her makeshift mask together.

This time, it was Mrs Singh who appeared, dusting her hands on the sides of her jeans before holding it out in greeting.

'Hello. Nina Singh,' she introduced herself in a twangy accent that looped its Ls a little too much for Mrs Roy's liking or comprehension. 'Sorry about the mess, we should be done in a couple of hours and then

I ought to get cracking on my groceries ... gosh, the day seems unending.' Mrs Singh offered, sending Mrs Roy into recoil, that someone would so freely share information with a stranger seemed exactly the kind of overzealousness she had a particular distaste for. She nodded her head in assent, and for once being at a loss for words, turned and climbed back up the stairs, leaving Mrs Singh a little nonplussed.

∼

Unbeknownst to the two women, their entire awkward exchange was keenly observed through the peephole, the other side of which stood Mrs Ranganekar. A reedy looking woman with a strength and industriousness that belied her structure, Mrs Ranganekar had finished more in the modest hours after waking than everyone in Paradise Towers put together. She had bathed, offered flowers and prayers to Lord Ganesha, brought in the newspaper, read the newspaper end to end, prepared breakfast for Mr Ranganekar (pouring only a cup of steaming, frothy black coffee for herself) after whose departure she had dusted and swabbed her flat, and tackled the preparing of food that went into the rows of aluminium lunch boxes, dulled from years of wear, that lined her kitchen counter. The Ranganekar home was a modest place sparsely furnished with what looked like second-hand furniture. No imagination was put into the choosing of upholstery or curtains and, apart from a large mirror that adorned one of the walls, there was no art. Sporadic potted palms dotted the living area and the only real decoration was a medium-sized stone statue of Ganpati playing the drums. A creaky pedestal fan was blowing the pages of the morning's newspapers, which lay on a small wooden dining table that was covered with a white table cloth that had brown paisleys around its border. One could say the only defining characteristic of the place was its cleanliness.

Within an hour of battling with spoons and pans, a fortifying vegetarian meal, generously portioned and low on spice and oil, had been ladled into the gaping mouths of the containers, stacked and fastened, now standing ready for pick up.

Abhorrent of the kind of polite chit-chat one was forced to make on encountering ones neighbours, Mrs Ranganekar stood glued to the peephole willing the ladies to end their conversation and leave the coast clear so she could slip out and hand over her steaming hot lunch boxes to the dabbawallah, who stood by the gate absorbed in the crackling commentary from the watchman's secondhand smartphone. A couple of minutes later, a rather furtive Mrs Ranganekar would make a dash for the gate and its attendant dabbawallah. Ignoring a salute from the watchman, she hastily thrust her lunch boxes into his hands, turned and skittered off as one would when a huge burden, not just in the literal sense, had been lifted.

4

The frenetic activity of the morning having been spent, the afternoon lay yawning before the residents of this marvellous modern structure. The mali, now dispensed with weeding and watering, planting and plucking his parcel of land, huddled down in a shadowy corner of the garden and, throwing one of his arms across his eyes, fell asleep. The watchman, after settling his lunch with a ripe paan, turned on the pedestal fan teetering on top of the famed register on a rickety, fraying, wicker stool, and sat down to observe the card game, being played on the bonnet of a parked car by a clutch of drivers whiling away their time.

Elsewhere in the building complex, Mrs Mody had been handed her post-lunch glass of Duke's lemonade by an assiduous Patrick, and was waiting for the AC to cool her room before she headed in for her siesta. Mrs Roy sat bent over one of her puzzle books, intermittently scratching her head with a pencil when faced with a particularly tough challenge and, upstairs, Mrs Kapoor was having her legs pressed as she reclined on her bed, phone clenched between ear and shoulder as she caught up on the mornings news with a friend, her hands busying themselves with turning the pages of a magazine. The Aly Khan flat was quiet – the family all away at the senior branch's house for lunch – but for a muffled cooing and giggling that seemed to be coming from one of the children's rooms. It was the eldest Aly Khan child, Laila.

Laila Aly Khan stood at the window talking into her phone and playing with her hair. Olive-skinned and lithe-limbed with dancing eyes and pert lips, she was the Aly Khans' first born and favourite child. Exhibiting a kindness of spirit that was praised universally, she took to helping her mother tame and monitor the rest of her siblings. It did not help her relationship with said siblings that she was held up in example, but she was good natured enough to laugh off their scathing protests against her, confident in their affection and reliance even though it was poorly exhibited. Now, at twenty she was in college studying to be a fashion designer and in the throes of her first romance. It was only a matter of time before someone fell madly and passionately in love with Laila. She had a pretty face that was enhanced by a lively and gentle character. Over the years, which only embellished her fine attributes, many a young man had fallen head-over-heels, but she had never found anyone of whom she could say the same. That was until she started college and her world was thrown open – and into it strode Aroon Sanghvi.

Aroon Sanghvi, heir to Sanghvi & Sons, a successful manufacturing concern with factories in three states, currently under the stewardship of his father, lost his engineering notes and his heart on the same day – in that order. The wayward notes had found themselves held hostage by a gaggle of college co-eds, who inherited the papers along with their table, and mistaking them for napkins used them to soak up a spill made when in a moment of great emphasis one of their number whacked her caramel frappucino onto the table. Serendipitously, Aroon happened to be on hand to rescue the soggy papers and the sobbing girl responsible for the accident. One look at Laila Aly Khan's flushed tear-streaked face and Aroon Sanghvi, owner of heretofore stout heart and resolute bachelor (at least till he was done getting his degree – first division, he promised his mother) was a goner. Always quick to turn any situation to his advantage, Aroon told a distraught Laila she could make amends by buying him coffee, that he had been in frantic pursuit of his notes and could do with a drink. Laila and Aroon got themselves coffee in a booth, which over the weeks was to become 'their spot'.

∽

Laila giggled and brushed her fingers through her hair. Aroon was full of stories, and this particular one was about the drunken antics of a friend of his, from the night before at a nightclub. She sighed; she had never been clubbing and when Aroon spoke of it he made it sound so glamorous, and so very grown up. Laila spent most of her time around her younger siblings and almost always got clubbed with them, giving way to what they wanted to do had become a habit. She must sound so gauche to Aroon she thought, and muffled her laughter midway through the story, clamming up. Leaning over, she reached for a cushion at the edge of her bed, hugging it to her chest. Being the eldest afforded her the one luxury of her own bedroom: a small cozy space with a single bed, which held cushions of all shapes and sizes and some of her favourite childhood plushies. A rocking chair sat by tall windows that looked over the car park, and a neat little bedside table, which could barely hold the books she was reading, jostled for place with a lamp. This room was the little nest she could escape to when things got a little too hectic, which they very often did, what with four siblings running around the place.

'Laila?' he said, she loved the way her name sounded when he spoke it. Lay-lah, though she introduced herself as L-eye-lah, he took his time rolling out the Ls and Is, as if he was sighing while saying it.

'Yes?' she replied dreamily.

'I ... would you, umm ... like to come out with *us* one night?' he asked, emphasizing the 'us'. She was unlike most of the girls he met, shy with a childlike wonderment about the world. He didn't want to come on too strong and scare her. She, he thought, was worth the wait.

Laila, stood upright, the mid-day sun now shining right off her face, 'Yes,' she shouted out, and then checking herself, in a more subdued tone said, 'Yes, Aroon, I would love to.' She loved saying his name, and repeated it to herself even when he was not around, sometimes she added a 'My' in front of it then, colouring up, would shake her head as if to dispel it. 'Only, I would need to check. Could I tell you tomorrow, please?' she asked with such earnestness it made him smile to himself and he closed his eyes as if wanting to commit these moments to memory.

'Of course. No rush.' He thought for a bit, then added 'If the club doesn't work out we could go for dinner? That is, if you're okay with it?'

It was Laila's turn to smile. 'Okay,' she replied in a small voice, her heart soaring at the thought of spending an evening looking into his face. How would she manage to eat anything she wondered, with him sitting there?

'Laila?' there he was again, snapping her out of her daydream. 'I better get to my next class. Call you later?' He did not want to hang up but his attendance since he had met her had been erratic and he still needed to keep his grades up. He held on to the phone as she said goodbye and kept holding on till the line beeped off, the numbers on the screen invading the space where her name was, in iridescent backlight just a minute ago.

࿔

Dinesh was pacing the length of the car park, kicking tiny green coconuts, which had the habit of prematurely falling from the trees surrounding the building compound, into the neatly painted rectangular borders that identified the parking spot of each flat. Every now and then he pulled out an oily pocket comb and ran it through his dusty hair, only managing to make the already static, stubborn strands stick up more. Oblivious to the heat beating down on him, turning his face pink, he would pat the pockets of his stonewashed jeans and matching shirt (he had spent a pretty packet on this ensemble, heavily inspired by his favourite Bollywood actor) looking for his mobile phone, and on finding it, checked the time, which in his opinion passed too slowly. In the foreground, he could see the watchman, nodding off only to jerk back into consciousness every time his head lolled forward. He cursed him under his breath, he would never dream of sleeping on the job and didn't approve of anyone who did.

A grating noise drew his attention upwards and he saw the window of the Aly Khans' flat open. His heart skipped a beat and he ran his now sweaty fingers through his hair, striking a nonchalant pose on one of the parked scooties and undoing yet another button of his shirt. Any minute now, he thought to himself, Lata would poke her head out, as she was wont to do at this time of day, and look down to catch his eye. This was the occasion that had inspired his sartorial flamboyance, a moment of Lata's undivided attention, a shared smile before she would colour up and, suppressing a giggle with her hand, turn away from the window leaving our home-grown Romeo delirious, clutching his heart as if to stifle its enhanced beats, hopeful that one day his affections would be reciprocated. However, it was not the lovely Lata that showed up at the window that afternoon but her ward Laila baby.

He watched as she spoke into her phone smiling and blushing, then hanging up, clutched the device to her chest as if it were a stuffed toy, twirled, threw her hands up above her head in a stretch that was borne more out of elation than fatigue, and continued to lean out the window humming to herself, breaking off every now and again to laugh. Laila Aly Khan always attracted attention, not that she ever actively sought it or in fact was even aware of the effect she had on people. She was always flushed pink in the cheeks, more an indication of her good health than any exertion from trying to commandeer her brood of siblings. Always in good humour, Laila's laugh belied her genteel exterior for it was hearty, straight from the gut and lit her face up; she looked like one of the goddesses from old comics, all wide eyes and lofty. 'What is this chakkar,' thought Dinesh, a girl has only two reasons to behave like this ... one: she has some good news or two: she is in love!

Pulling out his mobile to check the time again – it was getting on – then realizing he had to rush if he were to change back into his uniform so he could bring in Mrs Kapoor's chai on time, Dinesh skipped off into the cool porticoes of the building, bookmarking this event in his mind with plans to revisit it.

მ

Dinesh's vacant spot in the car park was soon occupied by a bicycle superfluously trilling its bell as Mr Roy, his mop of wiry black hair ruffled by the wind, and thick, black square-framed spectacles balanced on the tip of his nose that he peered over, swerved into place. Dismounting his cycle with some difficulty – seeing as he had wedged under his arm a briefcase – Mr Roy parked his ride, smoothed his clothes and hair by running a hand over them, pushed his spectacles back up his nose and proceeded to remove something wrapped in layers of newspaper from the basket attached to the front of his cycle. From the shadows, a middle-aged man came forward and relived Mr Roy of his briefcase, leaving the gentleman to better hold his newspaper-wrapped parcel. Though the Roy's had a car, Mr Roy preferred to use his bicycle on trips to the fish market, or so he told his friends. The truth however, was that he had once driven himself into the gutter right outside the building; a nostalgic song on the radio had set him off daydreaming causing him to lose control of his car. The car and Mr Roy were extricated from the gutter with great difficulty – one of the Kapoor children had even captured the entire episode on their phone. The car, though sent for an overhaul, would always smell of rotting bananas every time the engine overheated. Mrs Roy had ever since forbidden her husband from driving the car when he was on his own and so Mr Roy had resorted to using his bicycle for most errands.

Mr Roy rung for the elevator that whirred and hummed as it descended, the liftman smiling his broad smile as he came into view. The grill of the elevator drawn open, the liftman greeted his passenger, who once ensconced in the lift became the subject of his over-familiar repartee.

'Fresh fish for dinner today, saabji?' he asked eyeing the parcel that Mr Roy was now cradling in his arms. Mr Roy gave a perfunctory smile that should have indicated to the liftman that he found his questioning impertinent, but in this case managed only to encourage him.

'When I was in my village in Bihar,' the liftman prattled on, 'We knew many Bengali families, nothing like homemade maccher jhol, saabji. It has been an age since I have had the pleasure of eating such delicately prepared fish.'

Mr Roy leaned forward, pressing the button to his floor, which in his enthusiasm the liftman had forgotten to push, and the elevator began its laboured climb to the second floor, where Mrs Roy would be waiting to receive the fish that only her husband was trusted to select from the mongers, in lieu of which he would leave office early using a made-up Physiotherapy appointment as his excuse. With a click and a jump the elevator came to a halt on the fourth floor, where the middle-aged man servant, now divested of the briefcase was waiting to open the elevator door and let his boss out.

The minute he stepped on to the landing of the fourth floor, Mr Roy's superior olfactory senses picked up the most divine aroma. Tilting his head backwards, and flaring his nostrils, Mr Roy shut his eyes and gave himself up entirely to the scent. He followed it as if in a trance, only to find his reverie broken when his nose smashed against the door of not his mighty establishment, but that of his neighbour's, the Patels.

5

Mrs Patel dabbed at her chin with the sleeve of her cotton kurta, the spray that fizzed and whooshed around her kitchen as she stood steaming her dhoklas had left her a damp mess. Her kurta clung stubbornly to her curves and her hair, frizzy with the humidity, formed a halo of ringlets around her face making her look cherubic. Exasperated, she walked over to the switches and jabbing one with her elbow, turned on the ceiling fan. Immediately sheaves of newspaper that were kept ready to help drain the oil from the freshly fried pakoras took flight, and just like that Mrs Patel's mood worsened.

A tinny rendition of 'Greensleeves' struck up as their doorbell was pressed, and Mrs Patel bellowed out to her husband to answer it and put them all out of their misery. Mr Patel, who had settled into his favourite armchair with a flaky khari biscuit in hand, freshly dunked into a hot cup of tea and at that very moment was making its way into his mouth, sighed and bit off the soggy bit half-heartedly. He got up to answer the door, reminding his wife as he passed the kitchen, that it was she who decided to have the doorbell programmed to this ridiculous ring. She ignored him, continuing to tackle steam, paper and batter in what looked to be a losing battle.

Now Mrs Patel had a battery of servants who could have relieved her the trouble, but after noticing this afternoon that she only totalled 5,000 of her required 10,000 steps as per her pedometer, decided to prepare tea in order to make up the balance. This endeavour, as most of her efforts to manage her weight, hadn't gotten off to an auspicious start. She was now five pakoras down (justified as taste tests) and was reaching out for a sixth. Mrs Patel was a stress eater and worrier to boot, which put her smack bang in the middle of a vicious cycle she was unable to pull herself out of. Having spent thousands on dieticians whom she hoped would have more luck extricating her from it than she did, all it would take was a cliffhanger on her favourite TV show, or the infernal tests her kids would be given at school in alarming succession, and it would all come undone, setting her off reaching for the farsan cupboard and the various fried and baked snacks that lay therein. The trouble was, she lamented to all who were willing to listen, 'Our Gujju snacks are so delicious!'

'The trouble is, Mr Patel, that your Gujju snacks are so delicious, I am always enticed by their aroma, so please do forgive my intrusion,' blubbered Mr Roy to a nonplussed Mr Patel, who on opening the door found, along with the errand boy carrying a flimsy plastic bag stuffed with wobbly packets of milk, his neighbour: eyes shut a gormless expression on his face.

'Do come in, my friend,' said Mr Patel ushering him in, then gave the hallway a furtive glace to make sure the coast was clear before shutting the door.

The Patels lived in what could best be described as controlled chaos. Their flat was a riot of things, mainly kitchen appliances and gadgets, many as yet unboxed, that Mrs Patel kept purchasing off television shopping networks. The dining table, once a circular modern glass-top design, the copy of something Mrs Patel had seen in a cousin's home in Antwerp, was overrun with fruits in various bowls and baskets and Mr Patel's briefcase and Mrs Patel's recipe books usually left open with a pencil keeping her place in it. The living room, that their dining room looked into, was carpeted wall to wall with tiny rugs dotting the area. Plush sofas were arranged in a semi-circle around a flat-screen TV, which stood on a glass stand. When not in use – which was seldom – the TV was covered with a lace cloth, presumably to protect the screen from dust, the Patel children or projectile food – from when the mistress of the house sat watching her afternoon soaps while cutting her vegetables and peeling peas.

On to one of these sofas sank Mr Roy, slapping his thighs and then rubbing his knees as if polishing them. Mrs Patel appeared carrying a tray of steaming hot pakoras and perfect little yellow pillows of dhokla, the sight of which made Mr Roy rub his knees even more vigorously. She started portioning out the snacks into plates while absentmindedly helping herself to the pakoras at such a rate that Mr Roy wondered if there would be enough to go around. Finally, his plate in hand and piled high, Mr Roy cracked a smile. He dipped his pakora into the pool of green chutney dabbed onto his plate by Mr Patel, and biting into it sat back on the sofa and closed his eyes losing himself to its taste.

Snippets of the Patel's conversation entered Mr Roy's consciousness, distracting him from the sensory delights his taste buds were shooting up to his brain like bolts of lightning. He was a man in turmoil, an intellectual preferring the company of his books to any person he had ever met, including his irascible wife.

Now he was compelled to seek the company of other human beings, especially at meal time, for he had grown weary of fish! If this fact were known to his wife or members of the rather close-knit Bengali community, with which the Roys exclusively socialized, they would accuse him of high treason. And this was why he had taken to appearing on the doorstep of his neighbours around teatime, taking advantage of their hospitality.

Satiated and too full for his own dinner, which was soon to follow, these moments of stolen indulgence were the highlight of his day, one wouldn't be exaggerating if one said his life, so little had he to look forward to these days.

Soon, the worn-out warbling of '*Greensleeves*' rang through the flat again. Mr Patel, expecting the children back from playing in the garden, called for one of the house boys, who having returned from his siesta, ran to answer the door. But it was the lean sari-clad figure of Mrs Roy that came into the Patel's sitting room instead, having much the same effect on the group as that of a cloud obscuring the sun.

After greeting her neighbours and stating the purpose of her visit – she was in search of her husband – she stood silently staring daggers at her spouse who, oblivious to her presence, continued to fill his plate and mouth only stopping to praise Mrs Patel's cooking, lamenting the lack of such finesse at his own home.

Mrs Roy, turning a deep pink, folded her arms and it was in hearing the familiar clink of bangles brushing up against each other, that Mr Roy was alerted to his wife.

Turning towards her slowly, he smiled sheepishly and began adjusting his glasses and wiping his mouth clean as he made to get up. Mrs Roy's eyes blazed as she curled her hands into fists, her nails digging into her palms, her mouth a rigid line. Not attempting to say anything to placate her, knowing things had gone well beyond that, he thanked his hosts and, bidding them goodbye, walked out of the Patel's flat with his wife.

They were standing on the threshold of the Patel flat, the front door firmly closed behind them, when his wife turned to him – or on him, as was later reported by the Patel's houseboy who after seeing the guests out kept his ear to the door. As the houseboy said it, with the flair and drama of a habitual raconteur, Mrs Roy unleashed a verbal assault the likes of which he had never before heard, reminding her hapless husband of a rather unfortunate incident where Mr Patel had insulted her by returning her Doi Mach, sent over on the occasion of Durga Pooja, many moons ago.

'Have you forgotten how they insulted us?' Mrs Roy said to her husband. 'That too on Ashtami! Not only that, the barbarian stepped all over my alpana only days after.' She spoke of the incident with renewed vigour, even though it happened so long ago that no one would have remembered, if it wasn't kept alive like a perpetual flame by Mrs Roy.

'That was many years ago, we should let bygones be bygones,' Mr Roy hesitatingly suggested. 'They have been good neighbours. Our Shaana spends so much time with their children. Let it go,' he reasoned with her. 'Besides, darling, the Patels are vegetarian, especially during their Navratri ... it was not an insult to your cooking.'

Mrs Roy remained implacable. Her eyes welling up, she pulled the end of her pallu over her mouth and grumbled into it between sobs. '... and my husband, going to the enemy's house. That too for food. Have you seen the size of Mrs Patel?' she carried on bitterly. 'So much dieting but have you seen her lose an inch? Is that what you want to become?'

It was on this scene that Sameer Singh – eldest of the Singhs' four sons, newly arrived from the States, all of eighteen years old and oblivious to the inner complexities of married life – stumbled. Had he been older, not in such a rush or known how indelibly this would have marked him down in Mrs Roy's book as a 'no gooder', he would have done things differently. For as we shall see he would soon be desperate to have

Mrs Roy's good opinion, and Mrs Roy knew how to hold a grudge. This not being the case, young Sam, as Sameer was called, flushed red from running up the stairs approached the couple with a breezy 'Hi!' both embarrassing and startling them.

'I'm Sam Singh, from the first floor, we've just moved in and are having a party, sort of a getting-to-know-your-neighbours thing, here's an invite.' Thrusting a cream coloured envelope into Mr Roy's hands, he asked him to ring the Patel's doorbell for him, and on the door being opened, rather promptly, by the eavesdropping houseboy, disappeared into that flat.

Mrs Roy stood quivering with anger, her hands clenching the invite tighter and tighter till her knuckles turned white. Her face was a mix of horror and disgust. She was in no mood to tolerate such cavalier behaviour from someone this much her junior. 'Jonglee bachcha ... no manners. What do they think if they have an American accent we natives will be in awe and tolerate bad upbringing?' she screeched. Mr Roy, dreading a scene out in the corridor where he was certain everyone could hear, used all his wiles to change the topic, or at least to get her to their flat where she could rage in private. 'Never will our Shaana mingle with these hooligans!' she declared. 'What has this building come to, allowing just anyone to move in. Money is not everything I tell you.' She continued, walking into her flat. And just like that Mr Roy's few minutes of peace and happiness were once again stolen by his wife. As he bolted the front door, he gave the Patel flat a wistful glance, picturing a plate of dhoklas with his name on them.

6

Mr Singh set himself up behind the bar, the contents of which he had collected over years, portioning out peanuts, tiny emerald-coloured wasabi peas and mixed savouries into little bowls. Then he poured himself a beer, sipping it with relish using the back of his hand to wipe away the foam moustache it left behind.

In the kitchen, Mrs Singh peeked under the lids of the steel dishes containing the dinner her new cook had spent most of the day preparing. Having not had recourse to help during her days as a soccer mum in the States, she would be suspicious of anything she hadn't done herself. But the aromas that wafted from the dishes met her approval. Reassured, she joined her husband by the bar, determined to enjoy the evening.

The doorbell rang, barely audible over the loud music, and Mrs Singh shouted for her boys to 'turn it down a notch' as Mr Singh let in their first guests.

Mr and Mrs Ranganekar tentatively stepped into the Singhs' flat, nodding their heads in greeting. Mr Singh, eager to impress with the delights of his bar, offered them a rare Japanese whiskey, which they both refused, after much nodding of heads and waving of hands, settling instead for mousambi juice. They sat side by side on the Singhs' American super-sized sofa, wearing the expression of errant students asked to wait outside the principal's office. Clutching their glasses with both hands they listened with fixed smiles as the Singhs talked on, waiting for a break in the dialogue to sip their drink. 'So Mr Ranganekar, what is it that you do?' asked Mr Singh. In reply Mr Ranganekar took a long sip of his drink and his host moved on to the next question. 'Are you sure you won't have anything stronger than that? How about you, Mrs Ranganekar?' he asked thinking to himself that if any two people on this planet needed a good stiff drink it would be them. These two need to loosen up, he thought to himself as Mr Ranganekar, replying for the both of them said, 'No no, thank you. She does not take alcohol.'

Mr Singh left his guests to go add a few more cubes of ice to his drink. His departure was met with relief from his two captives, but not for long because as they sat back on the sofa Mrs Mody was making her way into the living area. This gave Mr Singh a minute to hang back and observe his neighbours. Odd birds, he thought and headed to greet his next guest.

The arrival of Mrs Mody, escorted by Patrick, spared them the ordeal of being the centre of attention as the only guests. Mrs Mody walked into the flat with a cane and the support of Patrick's arm. She paused in the corridor leading to the living room, held up her pince-nez, and gave the Singhs a once over. Suitably satisfied by what she saw, she made her way into the living area. She lightened up on seeing the Ranganekars, whose expressions in the interlude had changed from acute discomfort to one of alarm. Patrick found her a seat, which she had him push closer to the Ranganekars. 'Ah, Mr and Mrs Ranganekar,' she said with an emphasis on Mrs Ranganekar, who was so seldom seen around the building.

'What a delight, one can now finally catch up with you,' Mrs Mody addressed the increasingly uncomfortable couple who again inched forward on the sofa. 'It's been terribly hot for this time of year. Mr Ranganekar, you must feel it most keenly, seeing as you are out at work till rather late on most days.' Mr Ranganekar drained his glass in response. 'These may be old, yes,' she says tapping her binoculars meaningfully, 'but they miss nothing.' Clapping her hands together, her arthritic fingers bent, she opened her mouth to continue before the couple rose and, with much pointing to wristwatches, said their goodbyes and left. Mrs Mody shifted in agitation in her seat, but was soon occupied with a glass of Mr Singh's finest brandy, forgetting her displeasure at the hurried exit.

The Aly Khans, minus Laila who had a college project to finish at her friend's house that evening, and Kapoors arrived shortly after, crowding the front door and spilling into the corridor with their number.

A cacophony of greetings and introductions later, the adults were ushered into the living room. While the youngsters were packed off into the boys' room where, after making awkward introductions, they quickly found common ground and grouped around computers and iPads, their heads huddled together like conspirators. Sam, being the eldest, muscled to and fro fetching his guests' beverages and snacks, which they grabbed without raising their heads from their devices. The Patels arrived next, Mrs Patel had brought a glass casserole dish with homemade lemon tartlets that she handed Mr Singh, instructing him to refrigerate immediately. She then bustled forward to meet her old friends and make new ones. Mr Singh, a little put out at being saddled with the lemon tarts –

and denied the pleasure of offering to prepare drinks for the new arrivals – put the dish down on the side table and forgot about it.

Inside the youngsters, now fuelled with camaraderie and carbohydrates, grew boisterous as two more joined their number. They soon started chanting for A.J., brother number three, to perform. Only too happy to have such a willing audience, A.J. started to rap. The room fell silent as the youngest in the group stared at him, open-mouthed adulation clouding their wide eyes. His repertoire once over, A.J. was taking requests, when the door opened and Mrs Singh popped her head in adding yet another body to their number. All activity briefly paused as Shaana Roy, the only child of the Roys from the fourth floor, walked in and stood awkwardly in the middle of the room with a book tucked under her arm, looking for a place to sit.

Shaana was a shy, awkward girl who greatly preferred the company of books to anything else. Though friendly enough with the Patel girls next door, she was never good with crowds. She spent her evenings sitting on a bench in the building garden, her head in a book while the other kids played football or cycled around the property. Their bicycles dragging training wheels bent out of shape from overuse and intentional collisions that for the building kids made up a major part of their playtime.

Sandwiched between Sam and one of the younger Aly Khan boys, who had generous amounts of chocolate smeared all over his hands that he absentmindedly wiped on his shorts, while jabbing, with the other at his iPad. Shaana was unable to free her book from under her arm, and sat frozen looking straight ahead hoping to avoid eye contact with either of her neighbours.

Outside, the adults, loquacious and lubricated with the excellent stores from Mr Singh's bar, had forgotten old grudges, and good-naturedly mingled with each other. Mrs Roy had taken one corner of the room where she was educating Mrs Aly Khan and Mrs Singh – in a most animated fashion – on the finer points of Bengali cinema. Mrs Patel, buoyed by two glasses of wine, boldly edged her way towards them, once there she took to nodding her head in agreement on every point Mrs Roy gave emphasis to. Encouraged by the new addition to her group, Mrs Roy turned her attention from her previous captives, and now spoke only at Mrs Patel, who only ever moved her eyes off her neighbour's face when she turned to reach out for the appetizers. Grabbing a handful of cocktail samosas, she held them in a napkin and took bites at frequent intervals till they were gone and she had to request Mrs Roy to pause while she foraged for more nourishment.

The men, having gathered themselves around the bar, swirled their drinks and discussed the politics of

living and making a living in modern India. Glasses
were drained and refilled, and the bowls of nibbles
dipped into after every few sips, were restocked at
least twice while they guffawed over GST jokes made
by Mr Roy, a chartered accountant by profession, who
in the aftermath of its implementation was much put
upon – not only at work, but also by friends and more
than one neighbour hoping for free advice. Mr Kapoor,
one burly arm up on the bar, stood throwing peanuts
into his mouth. As the evening wore on, his aim began
lacking precision, and more often than not the nuts
ended up nestled on the painstakingly backcombed
hairs of Mrs Mody's head. The wily septuagenarian
had as her partner Mrs Kapoor, who she waylaid at
the beginning of the evening and refused to release
back to her friends. They were presently absorbed in
admiring the beautiful pearl brooch Mrs Mody was
wearing, a family heirloom that her ancestors brought
with them to India when they left Persia. 'Their lustre
is unmatched, not like what you get these days,' she
said dabbing at her coral mouth with a handkerchief
and curling it inside her palm as she held up her plate
to pick at a kebab wondering when, if at all, dinner
would be served.

Suddenly the lights were dimmed and the music,
old Hindi film numbers from the seventies, got louder.

Mrs Mody put her glasses on, the better to see Mrs Aly Khan lead her husband on to a hurriedly cleared space in the middle of the living room, where they begin to jive. A circle formed around them as they expertly pulled and twirled each other. Inspired by their ease and grace, Mr Kapoor dusted the crumbs from his hands and pulled his wife on to what was now the dance floor.

The circle got more animated as people, divesting themselves of their glasses, started to clap and whistle.

Mr Singh, thrilled that his party was a success, went over and stood by his wife, putting his arm affectionately around her shoulder, silently congratulating himself on the decision of moving his family back home. A sharp pinch to his backside snapped him out of his daydream and he turned his head to find his youngest, accompanied by a new friend, grimacing while rubbing his rumbling tummy with a tiny hand: the universal sign for 'feed me'. 'In a bit, bete, go back inside and play with your friend,' he said, brushing the little ones off. On their way back, the boys helped themselves to Mrs Patel's lemon tarts, taking as many as their hands could carry. Barely inside they were sent running out to smuggle in more of the tarts, as ordered by the older kids. Fuelled by sugar, the little ones crept back into the living room and started to steal sips from all the abandoned glasses, the adults too absorbed amongst themselves to notice. Drunk off of the contraband beer and whiskey, their mouths puckered with little wet, tell-tale signs of their bacchanal, they performed frenzied imitations of the adults, collapsing in hysterics.

Inside the kitchen the Singhs' cook, arms folded against her chest, was in a standoff with Patrick. He was, thanks to libations from his trusty little hip flask – a gift from the late Mr Mody – insisting he be served dinner. After a botched attempt at lurching for the tandoori chicken, that she responded to swiftly with a rolling pin, he abandoned all attempts and sat in a corner mumbling to himself about the poor quality of staff these days.

The thumps and twangs of revelry spilled out of the Singhs' apartment. On the other side of the landing, the Ranganekars had wedged a rolled towel under their front door to absorb the noise and were plugging their ears with cotton wool as they prepared for bed.

The liftman, who had been parked on the first floor for the entirety of the evening – no doubt to get first-hand news of the goings on – was perched on his stool, tapping to the tunes from within. Ever so often, he reached into his pocket to squeeze some chewing tobacco between his palms before stuffing it under his bottom lip. Then in a system that included exaggerated movement of his jaw to the accompaniment of some strange sucking sounds, continued to relish his fix.

Having worked up quite an appetite, the Singhs' guests now filed into the dining room. A large table, laid out as a buffet bearing steaming dishes that fogged up Mr Roy's glasses, awaited them.

Mrs Singh was putting the finishing touches to the candles on a rather modern, geometric candelabra. This grabbed Mr Patel's attention (he later told his wife he was fascinated at how the candles managed to stay upright, seeing as there was no real foundation for them) and in standing to admire them he held up the line, delaying access to the food. Finally persuaded to move on, he picked up a plate from the sideboard, where they were elegantly stacked sandwiched by thick paper napkins – which had the American flag printed on them with 'Happy 4th' embossed in red letters around the edges.

Slowly the guests circled the table and helped themselves to the food, cooing in delight at a particular delicacy, the ladies exclaiming that they 'just must have the recipe'.

Mrs Mody's arrival at the buffet caused a minor fuss as the biryani was hastily moved and given to Mr Roy to hold. A mat and cutlery were placed and a chair drawn up for the old lady to sit. Mr Roy, lost to the rich aromas of his burden, was nudged from his stupor by his wife, who grabbed the dish and, with some difficulty, placed it in the middle of the table – out his reach.

Mr Kapoor, always one to spot an opportunity, bamboozled his way through a knot of guests with a full plate in one hand, a dining chair in the other. He sidled up to Mrs Mody and, in a booming voice, declared to the startled lady, 'Mrs Mody, I shall keep you company, we cannot have you sitting on your lonesome.' Making place for himself on the table next to her, and putting down his tumbler of whiskey, cubes of ice tinkling, began to tuck into his dinner with his hands. Mrs Mody grimaced and held her napkin up to her mouth, shielding herself, as Mr Kapoor continued to spit as he engaged her in conversation.

On the other end of the dining room, Mrs Patel stood in front of a glass bowl, the contents of which she seemed unfamiliar with. 'Oh, my dear, this is homemade butter?' Mrs Singh giggled and answered, 'My husband cannot have a meal without it.' Mrs Patel seemed even more puzzled then. She had never in her life come across that much butter, and mentally calculated its calorific content. She spent the remainder of the evening taking sidelong glances at Mr Singh, wondering how he hadn't keeled over with a heart attack yet.

The front doorbell rang and Sam and A.J. rushed to answer it, relieving the delivery boy of his pizza boxes, stacked high enough to obscure his face. Sam gingerly handed him some money and made to close the door when he heard: 'These will not do, sir.' Sam turned back to him nonplussed. 'Last I checked it was Indian money, brother. What's the problem?' he asked testily.

'They are fake notes, sir,' said the delivery boy, holding a 2,000-Rupee note to the ceiling light in the landing. A visibly embarrassed Sam apologized, mentally making a note to tell his father. He pulled out a weather-beaten wallet from his back pocket, removing fresh bills and handing it over to the delivery boy, who on ascertaining their legitimacy wished the boys goodnight and left.

The two Singh boys looked at each other, bewildered at what just happened, but sounds of mirth from their bedroom distracted them. They headed to their room with the pizza. Kicking the room door open they put down the boxes, throwing them open and filling the room with the aroma of synthetic cheese and damp cardboard. In a Pavlovian response, the indolent bodies that lay sprawled all over the room sprang up and made for the boxes, grabbing slices, disentangling themselves from gooey strands of cheese.

Shaana waited her turn before pulling out a piece and returning to her spot where, in an attempt to rip open a sachet of chilli flakes, she managed to drop its contents all over the bed. The starting off a fit of sneezing through the room as groans of 'Shaana!' echoed with them. One of the younger kids, sticking a finger – previously engaged in digging out a jalapeno from the cheese – into his eyes soon began howling. The room went silent, and the older children, fearing the dissolution of their party, cupped a hand around his mouth hoping to muffle the sound. This made matters worse before one of the Patel girls managed to cajole the yelper into the bathroom where she splashed cold water on his face. The burning abated, as did the crying. However, the little tyke gave in to his inherently mischievous nature by splashing the water over his rescuer. She squealed and retaliated in kind, and somewhere between that, there broke out a water fight.

Sodden and manic, the children ran over beds and sofas, hitting each other with pillows, running to fill empty cans of Coke with water and launching them on the others. One of the little Kapoors twisted her ankle and fell off the bed. In excruciating pain, she limped to the door and entered Adult Land.

Mrs Kapoor, the first to spot her bedraggled and glassy-eyed daughter, got to her immediately. The little girl, whose ration of courage was completely depleted, began weeping while informing her mother in between gulps of air about how she came to be injured.

Most of the adults had gathered around the girl, making her even more uncomfortable. Mrs Kapoor, a little embarrassed by the scene her child created and concerned about her injury, caught her husband's eye signalling him to leave. The Kapoors gathered their progeny and after giving profuse thanks and promises for a repeat, 'but at our place this time', left. Their departure prompted everyone to look at their phone screens and declare they'd lost track of time and should prevail on their host's hospitality no longer.

The youngsters, all calm with beatific expressions on their faces, left their friends reluctantly. This distressed Mrs Patel, who as each unit headed out the door reasoned, 'But what about dessert, you haven't even tried my lemon tart?' The invitees, patting their stomachs, insisted they couldn't eat a bite more, except for Mrs Mody – who on her way out on the arm of a doddering Patrick requested for her lemon tarts to be packed. 'I shall send Patrick up for them immediately.' Before she got into the lift, she turned to Mrs Patel and said, 'Be generous with the portions. My parrot loves desserts.' She then pointed to her teeth explaining how she eschews anything hard in favour of her pet as her dentures did not allow for it.

Stifling a giggle, Mrs Singh turned to go find the tarts only to discover an empty casserole dish and lying next to it, fast asleep on the living room sofa – two little boys.

7

The morning after the Singhs' housewarming party was like any other. By 8 a.m., the sun was hot enough to steam up the concrete driveway, which the mali had just finished hosing down. He stood now in the garden, a thin red, faded, cotton scarf wrapped around his head; his pants rolled up as he waded in and out of the bushes, gathering dry leaves and throwing them into a wicker basket. The dhobi and his wife, after salaaming the watchman at the gate – he balancing a huge Madras-print cloth bundle on his head, she balancing hers on the hip – made their way to the staircase. They would proceed to stop by every apartment, untie their pile just by the front door and return, duly washed and pressed, the clothes they had laundered. Sometimes they would be pressed upon for tea, which they would hurriedly sip, while sitting on their haunches. At some doors, the chattier memsahibs would indulge them in conversation, mainly gossip from within the building and the others in the neighbourhood that made up their beat – all while ticking off the tally of items given and brought back on little hardbound register books.

Mrs Mody sat in front of the large mirror on her dressing table putting the finishing touches to her make-up. She forced her wedding ring onto her finger with the help of a little Pond's cold cream. Then, pulling out a frosted pink lipstick, she ran it over her lips, smacking them together when done. Next, she took a freshly ironed white handkerchief and, bringing it to her nose, took a long deep sniff. Checking to see if it was sprayed with her favourite eau de cologne – English lavender by Yardley – the very first gift her husband had given her, and the only perfume she ever used. Mrs Mody didn't care for perfumes, she felt they camouflaged smells, which was misleading. 'You never know what you can pick up from a scent,' she would say.

Folding the hanky into a neat square, with unsteady hands, she put it into her skirt pocket and lifting her walking stick, tapped the floor with it. When the sound failed to summon Patrick, she called for him. A jaunty Patrick emerged from the kitchen and, helping his mistress onto her feet, walked her to the dining room, pulling out a chair for her at the table. Sitting down, Mrs Mody gave a sharp nod, at which Patrick, tying a napkin around her neck to shield the front of her blouse, got down to the business of buttering toast. He then brought in the daily papers, turning straight to the obituaries, which he read aloud.

Mrs Mody stopped eating and listened. Relieved that no one she knew had decided to better acquaint themselves with their maker today. She instructed Patrick to clear her breakfast and hang her mourning clothes back into the closet. Reaching out for a little silver bell, placed on the table by the salt and pepper shaker, she rang it. Her cook, a pleasant-looking middle-aged lady, entered while wiping her hands on her apron. Mrs Mody enquired about the whereabouts of the promised lemon tarts from the night before. On being told they'd received none, Mrs Mody clucked, shaking her head in disgust and got up from the table.

Making her way to the balcony where her pet parrot – the object of her undying affection – was perched, she knocked on the cage, waking him. After a few minutes of conversation that left neither the parrot nor Mrs Mody any wiser, the old lady shuffled to her favourite seat on the balcony. Raising her binoculars to her eyes, she gave the compound a once over. Finding nothing untoward, or of any particular interest, she let them hang around her neck and picked up her cordless phone. Pulling out a smart leather phonebook from her handbag, she flipped its yellowing pages till she found the number of her bookmaker, or 'bookie' as she called him. The rest of her morning was spent on the phone placing bets. Mrs Mody was always lucky when it came to the horses.

Elsewhere in the building, Mrs Patel's morning had gotten off to a bad start. Waking to a terrible headache, compounded by the sounds of children fighting, she tried going back to sleep. Failing miserably, she made her way to the kitchen. The pressure cooker was hissing and rattling as her cook steamed idlis for breakfast. Mrs Patel opened the fridge and, pulling out a bottle of cold water, held it to her eyes hoping to ease the pressure building in her pounding head. Then, pouring herself a glass and fetching a bottle of Eno from the cabinet, spooned and stirred it into the water and gulped it down. She – even by her own standards – had overindulged last night and Punjabi food, so heavy on spices and oil, was too much for her constitution. The food reminded her of the recipes she had taken down from her neighbour. She tore off into the bedroom, pulling open drawers till they were found. Kissing them with joy, she inhaled the rich aromas from last night's cooking that the sheets of paper gave off. Her stomach protested and she felt bilious again. Lying back on her bed, she threw an arm over her eyes and tapped her toes together till the maid brought in her bed tea – tea, milk, two spoons of sugar, biscuits to dunk and whatever was made for breakfast any given morning. She ate her breakfast, keeping an eye on the horoscopes in the newspaper. It wasn't until she had read the predictions for every member of her family that she put it away, stretching out on her bed again with instructions to be woken only before lunch.

Mrs Kapoor was up bright and early – having spent the night in her injured child's bed, she was spared Mr Kapoor's amorous advances as well as his not-unsubstantial snoring. After quickly dispensing with a call from her mother, whom she avoided telling about her grandchild's mishap, she dialled her friend Mrs Aly Khan, and finding the lady awake and almost done with her house chores, sat down for a chat.

'What a success the dinner was,' she gushed.

'Everyone came, even the Ranganekars. I didn't get to meet them but I have it on authority from Mrs Patel, who knows everything,' said Mrs Aly Khan.

'The food was excellent. Did Mrs Singh make it herself?'

'They have a very good cook. I wonder how much they pay her? I should ask her to find me one.'

'And the Singhs! What a lovely family.'

'Even the boys. Not at all like other NRIs looking down their noses at everyone.'

'... and only drinking mineral water!'

Having agreed on the suitability of their newest neighbour they proceeded to discuss more mundane domestic issues.

Ending the call after a brief catch up on the happenings in Bollywood, as per the morning papers, Dinesh, who for the length of the chat busied himself dusting a particular table, with much attention to detail. On the ending of the call with nary a mention of Lata, abruptly abandoned what just minutes before had taken up all his concentration.

Shaana Roy was all aflutter, having turned the contents of her room upside down she was no closer to finding her mobile phone. She paced frantically about her room, a steady panic rising in her throat, making it difficult to swallow. Try as she might, she couldn't retrace her steps. In an effort to calm her nerves she grabbed a book. Opening it and dusting the crumbs that had found their way between its pages, she wondered if she had forgotten her phone at the Singhs' flat last night. Jumping into a pair of sneakers, neglecting their undone laces, she ran out of the door. She was rushing down the stairs that led from her flat to the Singhs', a floor below, when tripping on her laces, she lost her balance. Glasses flying off her face, she fell rolling down the steps and landing in a heap. After the initial shock wore off, Shaana lifted her head and rubbed her eyes, attempting to move. But a sharp pain in her leg prevented her from doing so.

Mrs Ranganekar was in the kitchen drying dishes to the accompaniment of songs from the local Marathi radio station. On the burner sat a saucepan, bubbling with masala tea. Grabbing the end of her sari, she lifted the saucepan from the stove, turning off the burner. Placing a neon-green plastic-rimmed strainer on top of a teacup, she poured herself some. Burning her tongue on the very first sip, she transferred the contents onto a saucer to cool, before she drank straight from it. Refreshed, she went back to her dishes, but her radio programme was suddenly interrupted by a news bulletin. The police were on the lookout for a gang involved in the circulation of counterfeit notes – civilians were urged to use caution when exchanging money and encouraged to contact a special hotline if they had any information. A pinched voice then read out the hotline number in a dull staccato.

Mrs Ranganekar stopped what she was doing. The saucer slipped from hand and came crashing to the floor, shattering. She was just reaching for a mop when another crashing sound – this time from outside – drew her attention. She went to the peephole of her front door and looking through it, found Shaana Roy sprawled in front of the lift that stood between the two flats on the first floor landing.

While Mrs Ranganekar stood peeping, debating whether to go to the girl's aid or not, the door of the opposite flat opened and Sam Singh stepped out. On seeing Shaana, he rushed to her, then retrieving her glasses from the floor, put them back on her nose. Asking her to hold still, he went back inside, returning a few seconds later with his mother and his three brothers. Carefully supporting her leg, they managed to carry her indoors. Mrs Ranganekar moved away from the door, wiping the peephole, which her breath had fogged up, went into her bedroom. A few minutes later, she locked her front door, ran down the steps and out the building gates, with a leather wallet under her armpit.

8

Mrs Mody sat staring into a bowl of chilled almond soup. Picking up her spoon, she skimmed the surface of her potage, scooping up the slivers of almond that garnished it. With an unsteady hand she brought it to her mouth and slurped. It was excellent, she told herself, made just right. She put her spoon down, savouring it. Despite the passing of her husband – it had been twenty long years now – Mrs Mody had continued to eat her meals in the formal dining room. A full silver service was laid out for both her meals and in the evenings, the candelabra: eighteenth-century English in silver with crystal bobeches. She believed that maintaining standards was the only way to keep away the searing pangs of loneliness and old age. Carefully finishing her soup, she rang for someone to bring in her lunch.

Patrick, after the excesses of last night and the exertions of his morning chores, had begun to flag as the afternoon came around. It took repeated ringing of the bell to summon him.

'That's the bell, Patrick. Mrs Mody has been ringing it for a while now. Would you care to answer it?' the cook said, sarcastically.

'Alright, alright I am going,' he walked out the door unsteadily, and whilst clearing the soup he was clumsy enough to drop a dirty spoon on Mrs Mody's lap. 'Oh, Patrick, I've had enough of your sloppiness for one day,' Mrs Mody said, angrily flapping her napkin at him, shooing him away.

'Send the cook in with my lunch. And don't show me your face till you can balance a tray properly.' It was a punishment Patrick was happy to accept. Taking up a corner, he made himself a cup of tea, livening it up a bit with a dash of brandy from his flask when the cook's back was turned. It was his habit to raise a silent toast to Mr Mody before drinking whatever had been helped along from the libations of his flask. And he did this now, dropping a little tea on the kitchen counter.

Mrs Mody made her way through the salad, and settled on her main course to the ticking of the

Ormolu clock on the mantle. She was on her dessert, a rich caramel custard, when the cook came out with a message. 'Bookie sir,' she said, was holding on the line to speak with 'madam'. Mrs Mody dismissed the cook asking her to tell the 'bookie' she would call after her lunch. Even her beloved horses, of which she owned a few, would not keep her from the rituals of the table. Mr Mody had been a stickler for convention. Telephones on the table, or TV dinners as was the custom these days, were forbidden. She preserved this custom, much like she did mementoes of her husband's life.

Theirs was an ordinary story. They had met at the right age, she just out of college, he already working in the family business. His aunt taught her piano and they first set eyes on each other while Mrs Mody was practicing her scales. Mr Mody said he was drawn not so much to the melody of her playing, but rather, her perseverance. He started dropping by to meet his aunt during these lessons and spent his time pretending to read, while waiting for her to finish. After which he would offer, at first, to walk her down to her taxi. As the weeks went by, strengthening their acquaintance and his confidence, he started driving her back home. Once he had ascertained that she felt for him the way he did for her, he spoke to their families and proposed. They were married soon after and honeymooned in Matheran. The only disappointment of their married life was their inability to have children. After trying for several years and failing, they decided to adopt one of his brother's daughters. The prospect at first seemed perfect, and a little girl named Shirin became the centre of their universe. However, after a few weeks of separation from her infant, Mr Mody's sister-in-law fell into a deep melancholy; it turned out that she was pining for her daughter, and the Senior Modys did the honourable thing by reuniting them.

Unable to cope living in such close proximity to a child that they were so attached to, but was now no longer theirs, they decided to move out of the family home. They heard of a modern building come up in the suburbs. On seeing the property, they fell in love with it, not least because it was a distance from where they used to live. They moved in almost immediately and became the first residents of Paradise Towers, one of the few high-rise buildings in the relatively uncongested suburbs. They were happy there, together they planted the garden that today was the envy of all their neighbours. They took long walks on the beach, which the building had easy access to, and developed a passion for horses, having a knack for picking winners and thus embellishing their bank balance substantially. Mr and Mrs Mody continued to maintain a good equation with their family, visiting them often. Shirin always held a special place in their hearts amongst all her siblings, and there were several. She grew to be a kind girl, doting on her aunt and uncle and visiting them often.

It was only Mr Mody who noticed that his wife had stopped playing the piano. He never asked why, nor did he insist she play, though listening to music was his favourite thing to do of an evening. One day he came home with a songbird in a cage. They kept him on the balcony and would sit and listen to him sing. When the bird died, he replaced it with a parrot, who mimicked Mr Mody's voice perfectly when given treats. Many years later, when Mr Mody died of a heart attack in his sleep, Mrs Mody would spend hours sitting on the balcony talking to the parrot, and if she was lucky, he would answer her cooing in the voice of her husband.

Her lunch done, it was to this seat in the balcony that she made her way. The sun had momentarily hid itself behind the clouds and a gentle breeze tickled the leaves. Mrs Mody sat, as she had every day for years, and sighed, looking out. From inside the house, Patrick emerged bearing a tray with Mrs Mody's Duke's Lemonade. It was a drink of habit, as a girl she was allowed it on weekends and only as a treat if she did well in her class tests. As she got older, Mrs Mody came into the practice of believing that it helped her better digest her meal, keeping her figure trim. It was a matter of routine that after every meal Mrs Mody would drink her lemonade and retire to her bedroom to sleep. Patrick placed the glass on the side table, where it fizzed and fumed viciously, and retreated to the kitchen. Mrs Mody waited for the bubbles to froth and eventually dissolve. She picked up the lemonade and took a few sips. Then placing it down, she dialled her bookkeeper, chanting his name aloud as she searched for his number in her book, returning his call. She was waiting on the results of a horse she had bet on, and something told her this one was going to win big. The phone rang without an answer and Mrs Mody, tucking it under her ear, cocked to one side holding the instrument in position, lifted her glass and drank, emptying it.

Finally, he answered. 'Hello, Mrs Mody, today is your lucky day...' he said, the excitement palpable in his voice. There was no answer. He tried again: 'Hello? Mrs Mody?' he said raising his voice a little more. But Mrs Mody had slumped over, her head flopped on her chest. The phone fell to the floor as the tinny voice of her bookkeeper kept repeating, 'Hello?' and again 'Hello?'

In his cage, the parrot – who had been pecking at his talons – became agitated, flapping his wings furiously and screeching loudly. The cage rattled as it began to swing with the force of the bird's distressed flailing.

The servants, just sitting down to lunch, rushed to the balcony on hearing this commotion. Patrick gently shook her shoulder, but Mrs Mody did not wake up. She keeled forward instead, doubling up on herself. Her binoculars fell to the floor and shattered.

9

A hysterical screaming rang through the stairwell of the building, prickling the hairs on the back of Dinesh's neck. He stood on the floor, engaged in idle banter with the liftman. Leaving their post, both men ran up the stairs till they came to the source of the screams, now joined by equally hysterical squawks.

They rang the doorbell urgently and a wild-eyed and frazzled cook, who up until a few minutes ago was feeding Mrs Mody her lunch, opened it. She hastened the two men in and directed them to the balcony where they saw Patrick, shaking Mrs Mody's inert body. All around them were fragments of broken glass.

In its cage, the parrot was frantically bobbing his head and flapping around, letting out shrieks that sounded eerily human. The men rushed to Mrs Mody, pushing a trembling and incoherent Patrick out of the way. Her body was still warm to the touch and a blistering froth had formed at the corner of her mouth. Dinesh pulled out a cell phone from his back pocket and dialled for an ambulance. Then with assistance from the liftman and cook he managed to carry Mrs Mody's body to her bedroom, where they lay her down on her bed, her glassy eyes staring vacantly at the ceiling.

The cook made to get her broom, but on the cautioning of the liftman to leave everything untouched, turned her attention to Patrick. The liftman stretched out a hand to the sputtering supine figure of Patrick, and on getting no response, nudged him with his toes. Patrick turned a face drenched with tears, sweat and spit to the man and grabbing his hand pulled himself off the floor. Using the heel of his palms to wipe his tears, he dusted himself down and on turning to look at the parrot, who had let up his screeching, burst into a fresh torrent of tears, lunging for the birdcage and encircling it in a hug. This startled the bird, who then took up his cries from where he had left off.

The cook, a hardy lady in both temperament and physicality, unable to understand Patrick's lack of composure, pried him off the cage, lest the aggravated bird start pecking at his face. Pulling him by his elbow, she took him into the kitchen. Once there, she filled two glasses of water, one she threw on his face in the hopes of calming his hysterics, the other she made him drink. After bringing Patrick to a controlled though catatonic state, she left him in the kitchen and walked out to the living room, where Dinesh and the liftman stood. She asked them to move to the kitchen, madam or no madam, the rules of the house were to be obeyed, and staff belonged strictly in the kitchen, not standing around gawking at the Modys' collection of antiques. The men safely ensconced in the kitchen, she went back to the bedroom to stand vigil over her employer's body.

The second time the doorbell of the Mody flat rang that day it signalled the arrival of the police. The cook, losing a bit of her equanimity on standing nose to nose with an inspector, let him in, displaying a far more subservient manner. Taking him directly to the room where Mrs Mody's body lay, now cold with a stiffness beginning to set in, she awaited further instructions. Following the police were the paramedics and his team – two wiry men in white shirts and shorts, little Gandhi caps on their oiled heads, who brought in a stretcher.

The doctor did not need to use his stethoscope. On touching the body and not finding a pulse, he closed her wide-open eyes and draped her with a white sheet. The men then placed Mrs Mody's body on the stretcher, and manoeuvred it out of her bedroom and into the living room, which was suddenly full of people and activity.

The police, now out on the balcony picking up pieces of glass and dropping them into plastic evidence bags, worked in a menacing silence. The inspector pulled out a handkerchief from his pant pocket and unfurled it, and then picked up the glass from the side table. Holding it up against the sun he looked for any discernible prints and then took a sniff. He called for his subordinate and asked for the glass to be recorded as evidence. A man in civilian attire was taking pictures of the destruction left in the wake of Mrs Mody's literal and figurative departure.

The inspector pulled off his cap and wiped the balding part of his head using the handkerchief with which he had previously handled evidence. On realizing that the cook was registering this rather disapprovingly, he sheepishly rolled it, fashioning it into a scarf, and tied it around the collar of his uniform shirt. Turning to the cook in an attempt to gain back lost ground, he used his most authoritative voice and began to question her about the events preceding Mrs Mody's collapse and eventual death.

On learning of the presence of another witness to the death, he asked for the gentleman to be summoned from the kitchen. A simpering, snivelling Patrick emerged and gave the policeman a salute. Spotting Patrick, the parrot, who having spent its energy had turned peaceful, took to rattling his cage again. It created such a din that the inspector was forced to have a constable dislodge the cage and take it to the police van parked downstairs. By the time the police were done questioning Patrick about the sequence of events that morning, word had spread all over Paradise Towers of the tragedy on the third floor.

Soon enough, a group of neighbours gathered outside Mrs Mody's flat. Some, like Mrs Aly Khan and Mrs Kapoor, were stunned into silence. Others like Mrs Singh were incredulous and a little guilty: what if the excesses of her dinner party were too much for the old lady's heart? Mrs Roy, who was making her way to her flat was the first to stumble onto the scene. Pragmatic as always, she made herself useful by vacating the flat of its visitors. Following that, she set to calling the next of kin, to whom in an even-toned voice she broke the sad news. That done, she emerged from the flat and bade the ladies descend to the ground floor so as to enable the stretcher to pass through the hallways and to the ambulance.

As the stretcher carrying Mrs Mody's body wound its way down the stairwell, people came out to their doorways to bid her adieu. Some, eyes wet with unshed tears, others in sober reflection, looked on in sombre silence as the lady – eccentric and irascible yet respected and beloved – left her home for the very last time.

A still windless evening followed the departure of the ambulance that took Mrs Mody's body from the building, to the accompaniment of a wailing, inconsolable Mrs Patel. Most of the men had left their offices early on hearing the news and sat in reflective silence with their families that night, resisting the allure of a work call or the headlines that normally constituted their evenings at home. Mrs Patel, having sobbed her way through an entire tub of ice cream, had retired to bed after a call with her family astrologer, who had suggested she perform a havan to ward of the ill effects of a strong planet that was unfavourably positioned in her house of health. He was naturally willing to take care of the formalities, saving her the hassle, for a considerable sum of money. Thus reassured, she fell into a deep sleep no doubt filled with dreams of the culinary delights the next day would bring.

Mr Singh stood massaging his wife's shoulders while in dulcet tones assuring her she was not responsible for the unfortunate demise of their neighbour. Mrs Singh leaned back against her husband and staring up at the moon, thought to herself what an inauspicious beginning to their new life this was. Her four boys, sensing their parent's mood would not be receptive to any kind of interruption or argument, had taken their meals into their room where they sat in equable harmony, watching a movie. Only Sam Singh sat distracted by his phone, turning it on and off in the hopes of a reply from Shaana Roy. A reply, that at least for tonight, would not come.

Mr Roy pulled the glasses off his face and rubbed his eyes. Turning to his left he realized his wife had not yet come to bed. Marking his page with a bookmark, a credit card-sized calendar from the Sri Aurobindo ashram, he shut it and pulling his blanket over his shoulders went off to sleep. Mrs Roy was in her daughter's room, combing her thick and rebellious hair. Holding the comb between her teeth as she began braiding it. Shaana, exhausted from the ministrations of the emergency room and a rather cumbersome and itchy cast, which now cased her fractured leg, was nodding off as her mother tugged at her hair. The braiding done, her mother helped her settle into bed and kissing her on her forehead, turned off her bedside light and left the room. On hearing the door click she turned around. Reaching for her mobile phone, she started to scroll through her messages. She re-read the message from Sam Singh inquiring about her leg and would she be alright with him stopping by to check in on her tomorrow? Not knowing how to respond, she decided to sleep over it and turning her phone off, did just that.

In the Mody flat, Patrick and the cook sat in complete silence at the kitchen counter dunking biscuits into their tea, having no appetite for anything else, and contemplating their future.

'I wonder why the police came.' Patrick said to his companion. 'Are they suspecting foul play? But Mrs Mody was an elderly lady … It is not entirely unexpected for her to…' he trailed off unable to bring himself to say the words. 'Who called them anyway?' he wondered out loud.

'I did!' the cook replied definitively. 'There is something about the way she died that makes me think it was not altogether natural.'

Patrick stopped fiddling with his soggy biscuit and looked up at her. Then drinking down his tea, set the cup aside before bidding the cook goodnight, and walking out of the kitchen. On his way to his quarters, a small but comfortable room at the back of the flat, he passed by his employer's bedroom. The bed had been stripped, washed thoroughly and made up with fresh sheets, as if expecting her to lay down to sleep in it again. He stood by the door, his hand on the light switch, and as was custom he turned the lights off and shut the door. Wiping an errant tear from his eye, he walked on.

10

Laila Aly Khan was fiddling with the car charms that dangled on the rear-view mirror of Aroon's car. They were parked a few houses away from Paradise Towers and were in the process of saying goodbye to each other. It had already been half an hour, but they sat fingers entwined, recounting minutiae from their day; anything to prolong their time together. '... and then?' Laila asked, for the umpteenth time, braiding her fingers in and out of Aroon's. 'And what, Princess Laila? I have told you everything ... twice over. My life when I am not with you isn't that exciting, you know,' Aroon laughed, bringing her hand to his mouth and kissing it slowly.

Laila lowered her eyes to her lap and teased him by trying to pull her hand away. She did not succeed as Aroon gripped it even tighter.

'Right now, at this very minute, you look beautiful,' he said, turning serious as she met his gaze. 'What did I do to deserve you?' he asked.

'You did nothing. I just feel bad I ruined your papers by spilling coffee on them. So I spend time with you out of guilt,' she said in mock seriousness.

'Oh. Is that so? Aroon asked, shifting his body to face her.

'Mmm-hmm,' she nodded.

'Well in that case you got off too lightly. I lost a whole ten marks for that paper.'

'What? You never told me that. A whole ten marks – oh, Aroon, I am so sorry,' Laila's eyes grew wide with horror.

'So you should be … *but* you can make it up to me.' He kissed her lips before she could move away.

'Aroon!' Laila screamed, pulling away. 'We are parked on the road not five steps from my building. Do you know how many eyes will be watching?'

'No, and I don't care. There isn't a time when eyes aren't watching you, Laila. And I don't blame them, look at you!' Aroon replied. Laila whacked him on his chest in jest and looked ahead.

She couldn't stop smiling. *How can he not hear how hard my heart is beating?* The rays of the setting sun shone bright, snapping her out of her reverie.

Finally, after running out of reasons to stay parked and hurried along by the insistent honking from a rickshaw stuck behind them, Laila unbuckled her seatbelt and, giving Aroon a rushed kiss, stepped out of his car and ran to the gates of her building. The watchman stood and saluted her as she, slowing her pace, walked into the compound.

She passed the garden where the kids from the building had gathered to play. One of them called out to her. She gave them a wave and continued walking. There was a time when Laila would muck in with the youngsters, leading their side to many victories in building football and cricket matches. But ever since Aroon had come into her life she was consumed by him, either talking to or about him, leaving very little time or energy for games she now thought of as childish – a fact that had not escaped the children's attention and they grumbled about her 'strange behaviour' every time she passed up an invite.

Dinesh, the Kapoors' manservant, got off the rickshaw that was until recently blocked by Aroon's car. He had seen the lovely Laila get out of a car that he knew didn't belong to her family or any of the friends who regularly came by the building to pick her up for college. Curious, he stood by the gate and waited as the car drove past, smiling to himself when he caught a brief glimpse of Aroon.

'So this is what Laila baby is up to,' he thought, grinning as he quickly pieced together the entire scenario. He stored it away in his head, and with a spring in his step headed back inside. This was priceless information and Dinesh had every intention to use it when the time was right and to his advantage. A muddy ball flew at him from the garden and catching it before it struck his face, Dinesh lobbed it back at the group of children playing with it. Among the smattering of bodies that ran around after the football sat Lata, in the periphery of the garden, pulling petals off of wild daisies.

Dinesh's heart lurched when he realized that she had seen him catch the ball and, pleased as punch with himself for the favourable light he had been shown in, ran his hands through his hair before reluctantly walking into the building as the children continued running around after the ball, screaming instructions to their teammates.

⌒

Inspector Godbole was cooling his steaming glass of tea by pouring it into a small saucer from which he noisily slurped. It had been a gruelling day. There was definitely something fishy about his latest case – the death of Mrs Mody – and he had been questioning the staff of the families that lived in her building all week hoping to get even the smallest suggestion of foul play. The death of a frail lady would normally have been an open-and-shut case but the froth around Mrs Mody's mouth warranted a thorough investigation. So far, he had made little progress. He twirled a multi-coloured glass paperweight and leaned back into his chair trying to clear his mind.

'What doesn't fit?' he asked himself repeatedly. After spending twenty years in the force and concluding more than half of his cases successfully, he was beginning to get irritated that this was taking him so long to crack.

From the other end of his cabin the parrot, that had been taken from Mrs Mody's flat, started up its squawking and Inspector Godbole, picking up a saltine from his plate, walked over to the cage. Breaking the biscuit into bits, he opened the hatch and stuck his hand in. The parrot fluttered its feathers and began pecking the crumbs from Inspector Godbole's palm. Having eaten its fill, the bird began to bob its body, as if dancing and then in a voice as clear as any human's said, 'Bookie 9-8-2-0-0-4-6-7-7-3.'

Inspector Godbole sat there momentarily, stunned and not believing his ears. He then got up and began to walk back to his desk when again the bird squawked out, clear as day, the word 'Bookie' followed by the numbers. Godbole turned and headed back to the cage the parrot now in a bobbing frenzy kept up a continuous caterwauling of 'Bookie 9-8-2-0-0-4-6-7-7-3'.

The inspector rang for a subordinate and on his arrival asked him to write down the digits the parrot was screeching out loud. The hawaldar did as he was told and then tearing the paper from the note pad bought it to his superior, who by now was sitting cross-legged on the floor, transfixed by the talking parrot. The inspector gave the scribbled words and numbers a once over, then throwing a cover over the cage, in order to silence the parrot, took the note paper back to his desk where he studied it for a while before banging his fist on the table effusively.

'I'll be damned, hawaldar,' he exclaimed. 'This is a phone number! Could this parrot have given me a clue to this case? Never in my twenty years of service has something this strange happened.' And saying that, he picked up his phone punching in the numbers the parrot had rattled off just minutes ago. It took a couple of rings before the owner of number 9820046773 answered.

'This is Inspector Godbole from the Juhu police station. Would you know a Mrs Mody?' The man on the other end of the line answered in an affirmative, and Godbole leaned back in his chair again, gesturing for his subordinate to leave the room, a satisfied smile creeping up on his lips.

11

A week after their neighbour's death, the ladies of Paradise Towers collected at the Aly Khan flat for lunch and to plan a memorial. As they sat around the table passing plates and dishes, dipping in and out of pickle jars, and crushing papad onto the steaming mounds of rice on their plates, they began to swap stories. This time, the discussions focused on the tyranny of their mothers-in-law.

'What do you know about mothers-in-law? Mine, I can bet, is the worst,' said Mrs Kapoor, her eyes clouding up. 'I was made to fast for Karva Chauth even though I was eight months pregnant. That too with my first child.'

'Regressive north Indian customs,' sneered Mrs Roy, whose mother-in-law had the decency to pass on before her son was married.

'The whole day. No water even,' Mrs Kapoor continued, directing the conversation at Mrs Roy. 'By the time we went up to the terrace to see the moon I was so weak' – here she paused for dramatic effect – 'I fainted!' All around the table hands went up to mouths gaping in a collective gasp. '... falling straight onto my father-in-law, who dropped me like a sack of garbage,' she moaned on, and Mrs Aly Khan bit her tongue to stifle a giggle. 'I was left lying there for ten minutes before enough people were brought in to lift me,' she finished with a sob.

The premature birth of her baby a good month after this incident, was linked in Mrs Kapoor's mind to this enforced fast, which she had been holding against her mother-in-law ever since. The ladies clucked their tongues and shook their heads in commiseration.

'I would never expect this from my daughters-in-law,' said Mrs Singh. 'So old-fashioned and cruel.'

'You would have four starving girls on your hands if you did, Mrs Singh,' Mrs Kapoor giggled. 'The very idea of so many hungry women in an enclosed space should be enough of a deterrent – old-fashioned or not.' The women laughed and Mrs Singh nodded in acquiescence.

'I, thankfully, have no such problem,' pronounced Mrs Roy proudly, looking over at her daughter, who had her nose in a book. Thanking her stars and leaving the table to wash her hands, she returned to it with her crocheting. As she burrowed her needle into loops of wool, her neighbours busied themselves with passing around plates for dessert. As rasgullas and jalebis were brought over by Lata, whose thin arms looked as if they would give way under their considerable weight, the ladies readied themselves. Mrs Roy, looking askance at the bobbing ragullas, screwed up her nose in distaste. On being offered a plate she turned it down with a brusque wave – no one in their right mind would eat those sad, rubbery balls made in a factory and passed off as one of the greatest Bengali delicacies! Picking up her crocheting, she moved away from the table.

Shaana Roy was squinting into a book as she sat by a window at the Aly Khan flat. Her injury had kept her from the school picnic and she was forced to stay home and spend her afternoon with her mother and neighbours. Tuning in and out of the gossip and chatter that threatened to distract her from her reading, Shaana slumped further down the couch she was on, and prayed the interminable lunch get over. The other thing diverting her attention was the constant flashing of her phone screen. Shaana was smart enough to turn the sound off so as not to invite questions from her mother as to who was messaging her, for the messages, increasingly frequent following the days after her fall, were from Sam Singh. Like Shaana, Sam was absent from school today. He was involved in a scuffle with a teammate and not being a good judge of his own strength had pushed the other boy, who landed on his elbow, fracturing his arm in two places. Mrs Singh was called to school and informed that Sam would be suspended for a week. Beside herself with anger, Mrs Singh had grounded her son, not realizing that he was more of a nuisance at home, where he was slowly divesting her of the contents of the refrigerator, and skulking around doors robbing his mother of her privacy. Just this morning, a friend of hers from New Jersey had called with major news: the daughter of a friend had gotten pregnant – the father was a gora and the captain of her high school basketball team, none of which Mrs Singh was able to respond to fittingly.

Never in his life had Sam Singh wanted to tag along with his mother to one of her ladies lunches as desperately as he did now. A text in the morning from Shaana had informed him of her presence there, and he chafed at being confined to the house when he could have been spending his afternoon listening to the soft sweet voice of Shaana Roy and staring into her big brown eyes. He had taken to messaging her all day, his frustration building as, today, she was being particularly non-responsive.

Sam:　　hey you, what's up?
Shaana: NM
Sam:　　hiiiii... how's the leg?
Shaana: same as yesterday
Sam:　　hahaha give a guy a break, I'm trying to get a conversation going here
Shaana: sorry, reading
Sam:　　plan on coming down in the evening?
Sam:　　we can hang out. I'm not up to playing football
Sam:　　you can tell me about the book
Sam:　　????????
Sam:　　yes?
Sam:　　no?
Sam:　　Maybe?
Sam:　　Shaana? Hello?
Shaana: too many aunties asking too many questions ttyl
Sam:　　damn! k! Knew I'd lose you to the kitty! ;)

Back at the lunch, the ladies finished their desserts, and after much malingering, moved to the sitting area to continue their discussions. Considering the lunch was for the purpose of planning a memorial service, little about its arrangements was discussed. Mrs Patel had pulled out from her handbag a little spiral-bound notebook with a pencil pushed through its binding and diligently wrote down the tally of what she had eaten for lunch. Her total count of rasgullas was four.

As the clock struck three, the ladies started to get restless, soon their children would be home from school and following them, the husbands. There would be school bags to empty, lunch boxes to check, homework to be followed up on. They wondered out loud what was keeping Mrs Ranganekar, for whom the ladies had been waiting a couple of hours. Finally, Mrs Kapoor suggested Lata be sent to the Ranganekars' flat to find out the cause of her delay. On hearing this, Shaana, rising to her feet with the aid of her crutches, quickly volunteered to run the errand, pleading with her mother that the exercise would do her good. Her mother reluctantly relenting, Shaana hurried to the door lest she change her mind.

The static energy of the afternoon leaving her as she exited the Aly Khans home, Shaana tried to navigate the staircase down a floor to the Ranganekars. A sharp pain in her leg forced her to call for the lift that came clambering down from two floors above, rattling its old bones on the way. Crutches first, Shaana stepped into the lift and turning around to face the front, gave the liftman a smile. Though relatively new to the building he had ample time to observe its inhabitants and Shaana Roy, with her quiet manners, soft voice and crazy shock of curly hair, was by far his favourite. As the lift came to a slow stop on the first floor, the liftman, drawing open the door to let Shaana out while telling her to take care of her leg, disappeared into the bowels of Paradise Towers.

Sam Singh could have sworn his prayers were answered when unexpectedly Shaana Roy appeared in front of him as he was heading out the door. His heart leaped and a blush started to spread all over his face. Shaana turned to him and wished him a shy 'hello.' Immediately, all thoughts of the errand his mother had instructed him about over the phone, were forgotten.

'Hey, Shaana, what brings you here?' Sam asked, hoping against hope she was there to see him. His spirits unflagging, even after she explained the reason for her trip to the first floor, he decided to accompany her to the other side of the corridor where she rang the bell to the Ranganekars' flat. Seating himself on the steps that lead up to the second floor, conveniently located right next to the Ranganekars, he beamed at her as she stood there waiting for the door to be opened. Even after a couple of rings, the door to the Ranganekars remained stubbornly shut. Shaana, a little nonplussed, turned to her companion for answers, but he responded by smiling at her every time she looked at him. Irresistible as his smiles were, for Sam Singh was a very handsome young man, it did nothing to help a very perplexed Shaana.

As she was about to turn away, the door creaked open, and framed within the faint light that shone through: Mrs Ranganekar. Shaana Roy's smile disappeared as the lady in front of her stood holding a tissue to her nose, which was turning red with blood. Mrs Ranganekar had a dark bruise around her left eye, which was florid as if recently hurt. Shaana stepped back, pressing on Sam's foot, and for a second losing her balance before he steadied her by grabbing her arm. If Shaana had been less shocked by the state of the lady in front of her she too would have felt the thousands of electric impulses Sam felt on touching her skin. But Shaana was fixed to the spot, her eyes to the floor as Mrs Ranganekar spoke in broken English, explaining how she had fallen during her morning shower, hurting herself and unable to make it to the meeting. Saying her piece, she hurriedly shut the door.

As she closed the door, Mrs Ranganekar turned to the figure of her husband, concealed in the shadows behind it, a witness to her conversation with the young girl. She jerked her arm free of the tight grip he had around it and went to her bedroom. He could hear her bolt the door from inside, locking him out. Walking into the kitchen he fetched a bottle of water from the fridge, gulping from it before dousing his face.

Outside, on the landing of the first floor, Shaana sat herself down next to Sam, and turning a pale stricken face to him said, 'Did you see her face?'

Sam, who had been unable to take his eyes off Shaana, shook his head.

'She was bleeding and bruised, Sam,' Shaana said. Sam knew he should be alarmed, but he was sitting next to the most beautiful girl in the world, holding her hand, smelling her sweet fresh scent. He could think of nothing else but Shaana Roy.

'I don't believe she fell in the shower. I saw finger marks around her neck. I think her husband is … beating her!' Shaana said. Sam rubbed his fingers on her hand to comfort her. 'We'll keep an eye on them for the next few days if you like, Shaana. If we see something strange again, we'll tell our folks.' Shaana nodded and blinked, suddenly alerted to their proximity and the public space they were in. She gently removed her hand from his and blushed a violent pink. Unable to look at him, she made her way to the lift – only to see it had been waiting there for her all along, the liftman giving her a knowing smile as she sheepishly entered it.

12

Three weeks after Mrs Mody's sudden death, the residents of Paradise Towers held the memorial. It came after much bellyaching and at least one fight over whether or not standing fans were needed to keep flies from the food – a disagreement that almost alienated Mrs Kapoor and Mrs Patel, and threatened to split the rest of the ladies into two groups.

The much planned and discussed memorial was finally under way in the building lawn. At one end was erected a podium, for the placement of which the residents of the building had to contend with an entire night of hammering. Many of the men, robbed of their sleep and a chance to watch the cricket match in peace, sulked as they sat by their spouses, staring vacantly at a large photograph, which was supposed to represent their erstwhile neighbour. Given the length of time the planning committee had invested in the project, it was surprising that the photograph chosen – garlanded with elegant pink and white flowers – looked very much like a passport photograph. The picture had been blown up far too many times, becoming so pixelated that Mrs Mody's face was unrecognizable – unless the beholder stood at the far end of the lawn. And squinted.

Below Mrs Mody's 'portrait', placed there by her cook, were the binoculars she had become synonymous with. Still in their damaged state, the tools of her vigilance lay surrounded by rose petals and elicited from her loyal staff sobs of grief. To one side of the podium stood a piano, on which the Singhs' musically inclined son was playing some of Mrs Mody's favourite pieces. As his fingers glided over the keys picking out the soulful tune of 'Sunrise, Sunset' from The Fiddler on the Roof, Mrs Singh's heart bloomed with pride. Mr Singh, on the other hand, was unable to hide his displeasure, that one of his boys brought up on weekly drills of catch and football practice was lending himself, that too publicly, to a pursuit of such delicacy. However, with his wife by his side monitoring his every move, there was nothing he could do but wring his hands in dismay and pray for the whole thing to be over.

The children of the building had occupied the last row of chairs, and sat there bunched together, whacking each other with plastic bottles that they had pinched from the refreshment table manned by Mrs Patel, who was swatting flies away from the edibles. If only they had a fan, she thought, she would not have to be standing here dispersing flies, she would be sitting with her husband, enjoying the music. She shot a dirty look at Mrs Kapoor, treasurer of this enterprise, who had opposed the keeping of fans anywhere in the vicinity of the open flames at the memorial. Mrs Kapoor was sitting by her friend, Mrs Aly Khan and sweating profusely. This brought a smile to Mrs Patel's lips.

A good half an hour into the memorial service, Patrick stumbled through the seated guests trailing a faint smell of hooch. It was apparent to everyone there that he was drunk to the gills, a fact that caused the restless youngsters of the building much mirth, and in the days to come they would re-enact with acute accuracy his faltering, swaying gait. The back row gave way to giggles as Patrick veered and lurched onto a sitting Mrs Roy, taking her to be an unoccupied chair. The sight of him, perched on Mrs Roy's lap crumpling her starched white sari while swaying to and fro, as she tried her best to hoist him off her person, sent not just the youngsters into peals of laughter, but had the adults biting their tongues so as not to join the inopportune hilarity.

The cook, stoically wiping her wet eyes before marching down the aisle, grabbed Patrick by his elbow and pulled him off an enraged Mrs Roy. Patrick followed the cook to the front row where he clumsily slumped into his chair, the cook's hand still holding on to his arm to assure compliance. He swayed from side to side, much like the palm trees that bordered the garden, which the Modys had planted when they first moved into this building.

A flourish on the piano signalled the end of 'Sunrise, Sunset' and many of the attendees looked at their watches – except for Mrs Roy who was busy settling the pleats of her sari and smoothing out the creases. Suddenly, a sharp falsetto pierced the silence, Mr Singh jerked himself awake, he had nodded off chin-on-chest during the recital, only to see his son, having abandoned the piano, standing and singing 'The wind beneath my wings' with gusto. It was enough to make his eyes pop out of their sockets, and he started up with a nervous cough, that only managed to draw even more attention to his person. Mrs Singh, reaching back, whispered for Sam to pass over a bottle of water, which she hastily opened and handed her husband, now red in the face.

As the coughing subsided, a sudden wailing replaced it, causing everyone to look for its source … all except for Mrs Singh's multi-talented son, who sang even louder. The wailing broke into hacking sobs and soon all eyes were set on Patrick, the source of this cacophony. Mrs Roy shook her head angrily and whispered something in Bengali to Mr Roy that did not sound complimentary in nature. Again, the back row broke into giggles, causing Mrs Kapoor to turn around widening her eyes in warning as the kids managed to stifle their laughs. Mrs Patel joined in the enforcement of a sombre atmosphere by bopping one of the boys with her electric swat, which set it off on a series of sparks and clicks, rattling Mr Patel's nerves.

The final beltings of 'You are the wind beneath my wings' merged perfectly with the sound of police sirens, and for just a minute the mourners were unable to differentiate one from the other. It was only when a cavalcade of cars drove into the compound of Paradise Towers and a host of khaki-clad men purposefully emerged from their vehicles that everyone realized something was afoot – everyone but Mrs Mody's loyal servants, who were both in the throes of heightened emotion.

The star performer of the evening, resentful of being upstaged, walked off the podium in a huff, noticed only by his mother. She engulfed her son in a bear hug, smothering him with kisses before he was yanked away by his father, who muttered, 'Enough of this singing, go join your brothers', and turned him in the direction of his siblings in the back row, who as he approached, made mock clapping sounds, contorting their mouths in caricature of their brother's performance. This earned them a punch in the gut, which did not go unobserved by their father, who suddenly looked relieved at this display of manly behaviour.

Meanwhile, the police led by a man in civilian clothes, marched down the aisle and came to halt by Mrs Mody's cook and Patrick. Turning a page from a little note pad handed to him by a subordinate, the inspector, tapping Patrick on his shoulder with his baton, asked, 'Patrick Gomes?'

Patrick, still under the influence of his emotions and alcohol, replied incoherently. The inspector bending to sniff the man's breath, turned to his subordinate and said, 'This man is dead drunk.' The subordinate, not sure whether this was grounds for arrest or mere censure, nodded his head disapprovingly. Breaking into this huddle of men, Mrs Mody's cook faced the inspector, and looking him straight in the eye, questioned him on his presence at their private function.

'We are here on police duty, madam.'

'Is this man Mr Patrick Gomes?'

The cook, a little concerned now, answered in the affirmative. The inspector then turned to Patrick and pulling out a pair of handcuffs said, 'Mr Patrick Gomes, you are under arrest for the murder of your employer Mrs Mody.' And saying so clapped the handcuffs onto a befuddled Patrick's wrists, to the accompaniment of a collective gasp from everyone present.

13

On a balmy evening, days after the ill-fated memorial, Dinesh and Lata sat in the shadow of an overgrown bougainvillea by the boundary wall of the lawn. They sat in tentative silence, turning to catch each other's eye and smiling bashfully when caught out. They left between them enough space for a third body. But today it was just the two of them, a hard-won date, testament to Dinesh's perseverance and Lata's ever increasing partiality towards him. A gust of wind brought down a shower of bougainvillea that Lata reached out and picked from, twirling flowers in her hand as Dinesh looked on rueing that he did not have the foresight to have picked some for her. Dinesh ran his fingers through his hair and Lata subconsciously mirrored it by tucking a loose strand of hair behind her ear. Clearing his throat loudly, Dinesh, his courage gathered, started speaking.

'Sad about Mrs Mody?'

Lata, relieved it was not left to her to start a conversation, and determined not to lose the opportunity to get chatting, replied with a shy 'yes' – a muted sound that was barely heard over the rustling of the leaves.

'Who would have thought ... Patrick,' Dinesh continued.

'Do you know the whole story?' Lata asked turning her face to him and finally looking him in the eye. He could tell she had lined them with kohl, something she didn't normally do. It struck him that she had done this for him and his spirits rose, his heart beating louder and faster.

'Yes, of course, I do. You don't?' he inquired incredulously; it was all everyone at Paradise Towers could talk about.

'No, not really, I don't listen when the memsahibs talk. Besides I have my hands full with so many children to look after.'

'Doesn't Laila baby help?'

'She does when she can, but now with college and...' Lata hesitated before bringing the topic back to Mrs Mody's death. 'Can you tell me about Mrs Mody's death? Are we allowed to talk about it?'

Dinesh's heart warmed, Lata was not like those other girls, sharp tongued and smarter than was good for them. She was shy and kind and kept to herself. He was no fool, as the eyes and ears of the building he was well aware of what everyone in its small community was up to. He had for some time now taken a keen interest in the comings and goings of Laila Aly Khan and, in particular, of the handsome young sahib who came to drop her, always two buildings down, in his fancy imported car. It endeared Lata to him more that she refused to indulge in gossiping about her charge, though anyone else in her place would have. Lata clearly had her loyalties in place, and Laila's secret was safe with her. Not wanting to make her more conscious than she was, Dinesh started talking, 'Well, so you heard about the police coming on the day of the memorial and arresting Patrick?'

'Yes, everyone does. Is it true he was drunk?'

'Blind drunk, he thought Mrs Roy was a chair and sat on her lap. Then he started crying loudly while Mrs Singh's son was singing.'

'O goodness!' Lata said, shocked that someone would lose their sense of station and respectability in such a public manner.

'And Mrs Roy?' she enquired, eyes wide open, anticipating the worst.

'There was nothing much she could do, thankfully the cook came and took him away. But Mrs Roy is not one to be messed around with, I tell you that,' Dinesh carried on his tone lighter as he got more comfortable talking to her. Lata giggled and looked down at her lap that was now filling up with bougainvillea she had collected from the grass. Suddenly Dinesh reached out, and picking out a pink bougainvillea from the ground around him, stretched out his hand to give to Lata. She giggled but shyly took it from him, making sure not to let their fingers touch.

'Mrs Mody may not have been an easy woman but Patrick had worked with her for years. It gives us all a bad name when a servant is caught doing things like this. We carry a lot of trust and after his arrest, my madam won't let me do the basics. It's insulting,' Dinesh carried on.

'What did Patrick do?'

'Well, he can read and write. Mrs Mody liked him to read to her after lunch before she slept. She was an old lady and a creature of habit. He's always looking for shortcuts and started crushing sleeping pills into her afternoon drink.'

Lata gasped, her hand on her mouth.

'Apparently, he had been drugging her for years, but had been clever about it, making sure he gave gaps so she didn't get immune to the dosage.'

'My god!' said Lata

'And I am not making this up, he confessed this to the police.'

'Do you think they beat him in jail?'

'Definitely, he needed sobering up. But they must have beaten the confession out of him.'

'Someone in my village got taken to jail for a petty theft, they beat him so badly that he is now paralyzed on one side,' said Lata, shuddering at the thought.

'Anyway, so Patrick was drugging his mistress and the time he got off from work he spent drinking. First he drained her liquor bottles and filled them up with local stuff. Soon, he started stealing money from her. He skimped on bird food and collected the cash. When that wasn't enough, he starting pinching the silver. Mrs Mody had no idea.'

'Funny that a lady who sat out on her balcony with binoculars knowing the wheres and hows of an entire building did not know what was going on under her nose.'

Dinesh looked at her and smiled. She was delightful, he thought; her shyness was easing up and she was interesting to talk to. Lata smiled back at him, a little more self-assured and bolder now.

'The night of the Singhs' party, Patrick had a lot more than his usual amount to drink. After he took Mrs Mody home, he prepared her hot chocolate and added a dose into that. Then again, in the morning, he was up drinking all night, he tripled his usual dose. She drank her post-lunch lemonade and was just dialling her bookie when they say she suffered a heart attack that killed her instantly.'

Lata raised her hand to her mouth cupping it as if stifling a scream.

'Patrick heard a commotion when Mrs Mody fell off her chair shattering her glass and binoculars and came running out of the kitchen to see her slumped over. He is said to have screamed aloud – "Lord forgive me, I have killed her!"'

'So he knew he had killed her? He admitted it?'

'That is correct.'

'He said this to the police? Why?'

'You won't believe it, Lata.' Dinesh hesitated, then suddenly said, 'You don't mind if I call you Lata?' Lata coloured and nodded her head in the affirmative.

'Remember I told you Mrs Mody was dialling her bookie when she collapsed?'

'Yes…'

'Well, the bookie was on the line, he heard the glass crash and Patrick scream out what he did. The bookie, not making much of the drama on the other end of the phone, hung up and forgot about the incident.'

'Then? How did the police get to know this?' asked Lata getting more and more involved in the story.

'It was at the police station. You remember the police collected many things from the flat as evidence?'

'I did not see anything, I was away picking the children from school.'

'Well they took pieces of glass, the binoculars and also the parrot.'

'Oh, she loved that parrot. My madam said it was given to her by her late husband, they had no children, my madam had tears in her eyes when she told me their story,' said Lata, a little sadness creeping into her voice.

'So this parrot, at the station, started speaking out the telephone number he had last heard. The inspector dialled it and it was the bookie's!' Dinesh got animated as he continued to explain the bizarre case of Mrs Mody's death and how it came to be solved. On hearing from the police that this was in connection with the Mody death, the bookie gave all the information he had. It was enough for the police to make an arrest.'

Lata's eyes were as large as saucers; she had never ever heard of something this strange. The death of an old lady at the hands of her servant in a case solved by a talking parrot and eavesdropping bookie. It was almost too fantastical to be true. She stared at Dinesh, her mouth wide open.

Dinesh laughed and snapping his fingers in front of her gaping mouth, said, 'Flies will get in.'

Lata, suddenly conscious, shut her mouth and rubbed the back of her hand over her parched lips. Then turning over her wrist she looked at the time on her leather wrist watch, one of Laila's given to her a year ago – her most prized possession. It was getting late; soon she would have to be off to collect the younger kids from school. She dusted off her lap full of flowers, making sure to keep the one Dinesh gave her, and stood up.

'I have a lot of work to get done upstairs,' she said to Dinesh, jerking her head in the direction of the Aly Khan flat. Dinesh sprung to his feet and walked Lata into the building. Before entering, they stood for a minute looking up at the third-floor balcony, now bereft of Mrs Mody with her binoculars and the parrot she adored. They sighed in unison and became suddenly conscious that they had begun mirroring each other. They both turned their heads away and walked into the building, their eyes firmly fixed on the floor.

14

Every afternoon, once lunch was done, Mrs Kapoor retired to her bedroom where she made her second obligatory call of the day to her mother. Mrs Kapoor's mother, widowed at an early age had brought up her only child singlehandedly. Her husband being a rich man, had left behind enough wealth for Mrs Kapoor's mother to live the life she had become accustomed to. Some shrewd investments and an instinct for the right stocks managed to double her net worth as well as enhance the young widow's appeal in the remarriage market. Many a suitor sought and was rejected the hand of Mrs Kapoor's mother, who was no beauty to begin with and her manly features and lumbering walk precluded any scope of enticement. But she was a rich woman and as all smart young men knew, looks fade, but the money managed by a clever woman only ever multiplies, and that was inducement enough. Mrs Kapoor's mother eschewed a second chance at settling down so she could focus on her one true love: her daughter.

Mrs Kapoor was an average child in every sense. She was average in looks – having inherited quite a few of her mother's masculine features – average in studies, always managing to just scrape through in her exams, and after she finished college at a polytechnic, she chose to marry an average man. Though she had her mother's blessings, Mr Kapoor was after all Punjabi and held a steady job, he was unfortunate in his place of domicile, for he lived in Mumbai. Introduced to her when he was on holiday visiting relatives in Ludhiana, Mr Kapoor took a shine to his wife-to-be. She was kind-hearted, got along well with his family and what she lacked in looks she more than made up for in personality. By the end of his holiday, Mr Kapoor had sent a proposal through his maternal aunt. The proper check into his background and bank balance having been satisfactory, Mrs Kapoor's mother conceded to the match. A date was set and so overwhelmed was Mrs Kapoor's mother with the building of a trousseau and wedding arrangements that she completely overlooked the fact that marrying her daughter to this man meant sending her miles away. It is no doubt that the distance would have done the young girl some good, she was overly dependent on her mother even though she had a good head on her shoulders and could navigate the nitty-gritties of life perfectly well on her own.

Now having lived ten years in Mumbai, Mrs Kapoor had managed to break the shackles that bound her to her overbearing mother a little too tightly. With the encouragement of her husband, she started to rely less and less on her mother. Quick to make friends by nature, they soon began to replace her parent as her advisors. However, Mrs Kapoor's mother was not one to be shaken off so easily. She managed, through manipulation – an apparently arthritic foot, which miraculously healed every time her daughter left for Ludhiana on an emergency trip there to nurse her mother – and a little emotional blackmail, by frequently reminding her daughter of the sacrifices she made to bring her up, ensured that Mrs Kapoor would continue in some way to be tied to her mother's apron strings. As a result, mother and daughter spoke three times a day where they would update each other on all things from the useful to the mundane. Mrs Kapoor's mother was an indifferent grandmother, her love for her daughter did not extend to her grandchildren. In fact, one would think she resented them for claiming most of her daughter's attention.

So, it was on this afternoon, while Mrs Kapoor caught her mother up on the achievements of her grandchildren at school, her mother feigned sleep, and yawning exaggeratedly into the telephone, excused herself for her afternoon siesta.

The phone call to her mother out of the way, Mrs Kapoor settled in bed, a magazine in her hand, and called out for the house maid. She arrived wiping her wet hands on her dupatta, a towel and jar of Ponds cold cream under her arm.

Now, Mrs Kapoor was not one to indulge herself in general – she rarely ever went to the hair salon – except perhaps that one time they went to her husband's boss's wedding anniversary party. She was not extravagant in her dressing, preferring the traditional salwar-kameez, she was house proud and preferred to divert any excess funds to the upkeep of her home rather than her person. However, if she had one indulgence it was her afternoon foot massage. She would sit back on her bed as her maid rubbed her feet with cold cream, which had that sickly-sweet smell of roses found in ittar shops in the bazaar. As her feet were being massaged, Mrs Kapoor would read film magazines and bring herself up to speed on the goings on in the lives of movie stars. It was to this end that the maid was summoned, and she immediately set to it. Laying a towel on the bedsheet, she placed

Mrs Kapoor's feet on it, and scooping a chunk of cold cream, she smeared it on her mistress's foot and began rubbing it in, her glass bangles tinkling as she went about her job. As the massaging worked its magic, Mrs Kapoor put aside her magazine, and throwing one arms over her eyes, relaxed into a short nap.

The maid continued to knead and press until Mrs Kapoor's breathing got shallower and she started to emit a small gurgling sound. As soon as she knew her employer was asleep, the maid pulled out her cell phone, firmly lodged in the elastic band of her pyjamas. With one hand pressing the prone foot half-heartedly, she used the other to open her photo album, and selecting an image – a garish bouquet of flowers on a deep-blue background with the words 'Goodmorning, have a blessed day' written across it in a cursive font in fuchsia pink – sent it to numerous members in her contact list. Then opening her WhatsApp, she scrolled down the many messages displaying photographs of puppies with angel wings or haloed kittens frolicking around plants. Mrs Kapoor's gurgling stopped and she shook her leg, a sign for the maid to press harder. Putting her phone away, she applied more pressure, and inadvertently pressing on a soft spot managed to hurt Mrs Kapoor, who woke up irritable.

'Watch what you are doing!' she reprimanded the woman and said, 'Call Dinesh, he is the only one I can rely on here to do anything properly.' The maid, eyes averted, continued without any response. Mrs Kapoor, snatching her foot back from the maid, demanded she go bring Dinesh.

'Dinesh is not in the house, madam,' the maid answered sheepishly. Mrs Kapoor's irritation doubled and she insisted Dinesh be summoned to her immediately. The maid left the room in a nervous hurry and frantically tried to locate Dinesh. The liftman, having just seen Dinesh walking into the building with Lata, and not wanting to disturb their romantic interlude, waylaid the maid, who had come to him for help in locating her co-worker. Once she left, he headed down to the ground floor, where he found the lovelorn boy and rushed him back to the Kapoor flat.

Half an hour after she had called for her servant, Mrs Kapoor, now visibly angry, was sitting on her couch, flipping channels on the television as a repentant Dinesh stood in front of her, his head lowered.

'Your impertinence knows no bounds, Dinesh. Don't think you are indispensable,' Mrs Kapoor reprimanded him, while still pressing the buttons on her remote. 'This is all because of that silly girl who works at the Aly Khans'! Don't forget you were raw when I got you to work here, a mere teenager. I've trained you, taught you how to drive. You should have some sense of duty. Don't let some young thing turn your head from your work,' she carried on, wiping the remote on her cotton kameez and inadvertently increasing the volume by pressing on the buttons. The TV let out a loud bark, which startled her and she quickly handed Dinesh the remote entreating him to do something with the volume. He did so silently before handing it back.

Her anger having abated some, she looked at him and asks in a more pleasant tone, 'What is it? Are you in love with this girl? I hope you are not thinking of marriage just yet?' Dinesh was alarmed by his employer's change of tone and looked up at her, colouring. He smiled and scratched his head. 'Dinesh, I hope you are not up to any hanky-panky, she works for my closest friend and I do not want trouble or any issues between our families. Certainly not on your account.'

Dinesh coloured even deeper, shaking his head to Mrs Kapoor's concerns about him being cavalier with Lata and then nods to her orders about avoiding tension between the families. Relieved to be let off the hook with a mere rap on the knuckles, he felt the need to reciprocate by rewarding his mistress with some choice information.

'Madam,' he said, hesitating a little.

'What is it, Dinesh? Speak up, don't act coy with me – I don't buy it.'

'Aly Khan Madam is your friend. I am but a poor servant, dependant on you for my existence. I don't know if I should be saying this but...' he trailed off, knowing full well that his employer and taken the bait. He paused.

'What? Out with it,' Mrs Kapoor demanded. For a practical, no-nonsense lady she had a huge appetite for gossip, whether it be the most mundane news from the building or otherwise. It was her greatest currency, she wasn't much of a looker, nor a rich woman, but she made sure she was the best informed and, therefore, an integral part of every gathering. Her news was never untrue and her record for being the first to break it remained unchallenged. She was irritated at being now beholden to her servant for information, especially one who behaved badly. She had wanted to give him the cold shoulder for a few days till he realized his place. She tried her best to be nonchalant about the news her servant was about to give her, but they both knew better.

'Madam, Laila baby madam...' again he trailed off, this time he wasn't playacting. It was sensitive information and he was nervous.

'Yes, what about Laila baby?'

'...there is a boy, madam. He comes to drop her every day, they park two buildings down. I have seen them many times. They sit with the windows rolled up and talk.' He blurted, knowing it was too late to save Laila – the sacrifice meant to appease his employer. Mrs Kapoor stopped playing with the remote and turned to face her servant. Unable to read her face, he prattled on, if only to rid the room of the sudden quiet that had him more nervous than before.

'Madam, he is a Hindu boy. There is a Hanuman pendant hanging from his rear-view mirror,' he said, unable to look up at her.

Mrs Kapoor, sitting with her mouth agape and eyes wide, looked out the window, thought for a minute and asked Dinesh to bring her the cordless phone. She punched in a number and a woman answered.

'Hi. Make some tea, less milk. I'm coming down. We need to talk!'

15

It was exceptionally rare in the Aly Khan home for there to be an afternoon without the to-ing and fro-ing of children. Having five kids to contend with, Mrs Aly Khan was always organizing either tuition classes or tennis lessons. The car was in perpetual use, dropping or picking someone or the other from school or classes or college. It was a huge relief to Mrs Aly Khan therefore when her eldest daughter Laila suggested she car pool with a friend to college. Mrs Aly Khan had readily agreed and Laila was given more autonomy than she had ever been used to. Today, as she sat sobbing into a wad of tissues, some of which littered her floor, Mrs Aly Khan regretted being such a fool and not keeping tabs on her eldest child.

Laila Aly Khan was a beauty. From the day she was born, she had stolen her father's heart. A succession of children followed but none could supplant her in the affections of her father, even the much-longed-for boys. Laila grew to be a gentle and kind-hearted girl, always polite and patient with her parent's friends or relatives, who pinched her pink cheeks and commented on her green eyes. She had always worn her hair long, like her mother's, but hers was shot through with strands of caramel that caught the sunlight. A generous mouth sat under a dainty nose and her complexion was olive. Overall, the effect was striking, but the girl seemed unaware of the effect it had on others. Many a boy had lost his heart to her but she had never reciprocated, not out of pride but sheer lack of interest. She was devoted to her siblings, adored by the staff to whom she was always courteous and helpful, and depended on by her mother, to whom she deferred on all things.

Laila knew her mother was treated with great disdain by her father's family and she tried her best to uplift her mother after particularly trying visits to her grandparents' home where Mrs Aly Khan was barely tolerated. She never resented the fuss made over the two brothers when they were given first pick of the gifts or more money than she was on festivals. In fact, she helped console her younger sisters who would feel the disparity a lot more and share her things with them to cheer them up. Everyone who encountered Laila Aly Khan wished her the best in life, which was why Lata also sat sobbing in the kitchen, being plied with water by the cook in the aftermath of Mrs Kapoor's revelation. Lata was furious with Dinesh. How could he have done this to her most precious and beloved charge? His name flashed on the green screen of her mobile phone. Lata turned it off.

Outside, Mrs Kapoor had moved herself to the seat near her friend's and was now rubbing her back and bolstering her spirits by repeatedly saying, 'There, there, it is the folly of youth. She is a good girl. All will be well.'

Mrs Aly Khan blew her nose on the soggy tissues. She looked up at her friend, who had just a few minutes ago given her the devastating news that her daughter, the meek Laila, was running around with a boy behind her back, and worse: the whole building knew about it. If her in-laws found out, it would be another black mark against her name, one she could ill afford. Ever since her brother-in-law, Mr Aly Khan's younger brother, married the girl of his parents picking a year ago, Mrs Aly Khan was slighted at every opportunity. The new daughter-in-law had them eating out of her palms.

Mrs Aly Khan, however, had the complete support of her husband, the eldest in the family and the most successful. No one would dare to cross him, but it was behind his back that poor Mrs Aly Khan had to hear taunts. She never complained to her husband and he was largely ignorant of exactly how tough visits to his parents' home were on her. That he was madly in love with his wife was no secret. She was pampered by him and he was loyal to her.

It was expected that Laila make a good marriage, and only on the insistence of her father that she be educated, was she sent to college. Every week the elder ladies in the Aly Khan family would sift through piles of photographs of suitable Muslim boys from good families for Laila. In fact, Mrs Aly Khan's new sister-in-law was keen to snap up this beauty for her own brother, a software engineer in LA and set to make a visit to Mumbai around Diwali. She was hoping to introduce the two then. Mrs Aly Khan transferred this information to her friend Mrs Kapoor, and told her of the repercussions of anyone finding out Laila was seeing a Hindu boy. She was so fearful, she could barely get the words out.

'Whatever you do, do not tell your husband about any of this,' Mrs Kapoor counselled her friend. 'Let us wait till the child gets home today and talk some sense into her.'

Mrs Aly Khan nodded and blew her nose for the last time, placated she bent to pick up the scattered tissues and walked to the kitchen where she handed them to a red-eyed Lata, asking her to throw them. She ordered another cup of tea for herself and her friend and asked the cook to fry some pakoras. Mrs Aly Khan always ate when she was upset and it was surprising she maintained a slim figure, for she was often upset owing to some slight from her husband's family.

That night, Laila Aly Khan stood by the open window of her room. She looked up at the fingernail moon that hung over the trees and beyond the passing clouds. Outside, the crickets struck up their scratching and trilling, and she could see people settling in for the night all along the pavement using threadbare sheets for cover. Beneath the window, the cars and scooters lined up in the parking lot were collecting dew on their hoods, making them shimmer in the reflection of the street lamps. Laila, pulling out her phone, dialled a number. The house was quiet and all her siblings fast asleep, well into their childlike dreams, untainted by the travails of adulthood. She was that innocent once, she thought to herself. Just a few hours back she was tucked in with her littlest sister reading to her from her favourite story book about princesses.

'If only it were so in real life,' she has time to say before Aroon answers. 'Laila you have me so worried. I got your message, what happened? Are you okay?'

When it is her turn to speak, she begins to tell the man, to whom she has given her heart, that her mother had found out about them. That she at first reasoned then reprimanded and eventually forbade her daughter from leaving the house or ever speaking to or seeing him again. Her beautiful face crumpled and reddened as tears streamed down her cheeks, which she wiped with the back of her hand.

'She hasn't told my father yet. Said that if I promise to break it off with you she won't have to,' Laila said, her heartbreak palpable in her voice. All Aroon manages to say is 'Laila' again and again, as if the repetition of her name will soothe her.

'I don't know what to do, Aroon. I love my parents. I don't want to upset them, but I can't imagine being without you.' She whispered to him, turning to check her bedroom door. It remained shut with the rest of the room plunged in darkness. She faced the night sky again and fresh tears rolled down, collecting at the hollow of her neck.

'Laila, do you trust me?' Aroon asked and she nodded before realizing he couldn't see her face and replied.

'Then go to sleep, let me think of something. Trust me, I'll figure it all out. Please stop crying and leave it to me.' He reassured her over and over until she stopped crying. There was silence before he continued, 'And Laila...'

'... yes?'

'I love you,' he said before they hung up. Laila shut the window, drew the curtains and went to bed.

16

Mrs Ranganekar finished her morning shower and emerged from the bathroom. A towel was wrapped around her wet hair like a long cloth braid, and the top of her head was exposed and wet, dripping onto her blouse. As part of her morning routine, she walked to her little mandir: a stool, covered with a saffron cloth, on which stood the brass idols. Pulling out a handful of incense, she lit them with a match before waving them through the air. Snuffing out the flame, she left them to smoulder, as they would through the day, giving off an aroma and the sense of prayer and piety. She opened a small newspaper bundle inside which were tiny marigold flowers that the watchman had delivered to her flat earlier that morning, as he had done every morning since the Ranganekars came to live at Paradise Towers. She placed the flowers by the feet of her miniature idols and then picking up a tiny bell by its wooden handle in one hand, rang it continuously while tracing little circles of smoke with her incense sticks, which she delicately held in her other hand, around the idols. This done, she joined her hands in prayer, lips moving in silent invocation.

By the time she finished with her prayers, her blouse was soaked through and she rose to grab another one from her cupboard before entering the bathroom to change.

In the bathroom, she undraped the pallu and gently unhooked her blouse, wincing as she pulled it off her arms. She looked into the mirror: her shoulders were covered with angry bruises turning a ripe violet. She ran her fingers over them flinching at the lightest touch. She stared into the mirror inured to the reflection of violence she had endured for a year into her marriage; she had now been married for five. Pulling the towel off her head, she gathered her hair into a bun and wiped her moist eyes. Taking a deep breath, she pulled on the dry blouse, hooked it up, and draping her sari, made to unlatch the bathroom door. She paused for a second, her forehead against the latch, before squaring her shoulders and walking out. She walked into the kitchen immediately to avoid communication with her husband.

Mr Ranganekar, in a white vest and checked lungi, was leaning out their living room window, smoking a cigarette. He could hear his wife busying herself in the kitchen and the sounds of her opening jars and lighting their gas stove irritated him. Clenching his burning cigarette between two fingers, he used his thumb to scratch his nose before taking a long drag. He closed his eyes on the exhale, and overcome by regret and shame he hung his head, his free hand clasping the back of his neck. The young laughing face of his wife flashed before his eyes, and in that vision they were sitting on the beach, the waves reaching out to tickle her toes as she handed him a paper cone of coal-roasted peanuts – which he had just bought her – and wetting her fingers in the water, flicked droplets at him. He laughed while wiping the moisture off his face. Her hair had come loose in tendrils from her braid and the salt air curled them up like tightly wound springs. He tugs at them just to watch them curl right up again. But he did not think of this last night when he grabbed onto her hair, pulling at it, her neck bent backward in an unnatural curve as she squirmed and begged him to let go. She had stopped crying, he remembers thinking right before he banged her head against the cupboard and leaving her to slink slowly on to the floor.

He could hear her clearing her throat behind him and turned to see her standing there with his morning tea. He took it from her with a wan smile. She did not acknowledge it and walked back into the kitchen. Inside the kitchen she opened a packet of biscuits and dunking one in her tea, looked out the kitchen window.

They had met at work; she was a steno at his office and he the personal assistant to the vice chairman. They began talking when she offered him a poran poli after looking at his dismayed face at the cafeteria table one day soon after he joined the company. The canteen food was inconsistent at best and he was grateful for a little taste of home. Mr Ranganekar had moved to Mumbai from Kolhapur, and was staying as a paying guest with a Gujarati couple near his office. The kindness of this young stenographer with a crooked smile and defiant eyes touched his heart. The next day, he brought her flowers for her hair, which she accepted gracefully but never wore. Six months later, when he came with his parents to ask for her hand in marriage, her father had accepted immediately. He was from a decent background and had good prospects. They were married without much fuss in a sensible ceremony at a wedding hall in Shivaji park. After the ceremony he took her to Kolhapur to meet his relatives and show her the town he grew up in.

It was shortly after they returned from this honeymoon of sorts that Mr Ranganekar's boss left the company for a better job in Singapore. The organization could not absorb him and just like that Mr Ranganekar was out of a job, and dependent on his wife's income. The first time he struck her was after a rickshaw ride home from meeting her parents. She had reached into her purse to pay the fare and Mr Ranganekar felt it like a slap across his face. So, when they got back up to their room, still in the PG he was staying in before he got married, he grabbed her by the arm and struck her hard across her face. At first she was silent in shock and then she jerked her arm out of his grasp, which angered him more and he struck her again. He held her as she sobbed herself to sleep that night, reassuring her it would never happen again. But it did, just a few months later, and then it never stopped.

Sometimes there would be a lull and she would think his anger had spent itself and he was back to the man she once worked with. Then it would start up again. First it broke her body and then her spirit. Then she stopped reacting altogether, taking his blows like an inanimate object. The next day was always full of regret and sorries but she knew better, knowing nothing would change. It was her secret and she hid it well. Her parents never guessed, she did not want to burden them with it. He made her leave her job at the company. It spurred his fury to see her set off to the office he was let go of from. She quit to keep the peace – a prisoner in the walls of her home.

The bedroom door banged shut and Mrs Ranganekar was jolted out of her reverie. Her tea was cold and the biscuit had turned mealy. She poured her beverage down the sink, but ate the biscuit anyway. It was all she would be able to stomach today – the day after was always the worst. Going into the living room, she collected the cup of tea her husband had left on the windowsill and carried it back to the kitchen. She was half way through assembling her tiffin boxes when he bellowed out to her.

'There is a tear in my shirt, why haven't you fired that dhobi?' he asked.

'It is not their fault, I should have checked,' she replied matter-of-factly without stopping what she was doing.

'I make enough money to afford dry cleaning, you know. I've given you this fancy flat in a fancy building, the least you can do is make sure I don't go to work looking like a beggar. Would you like your husband to be embarrassed?'

'What work,' she mumbled under her breath, out of his hearing and then said, louder: 'It won't happen again, take another one. I have hung a few up in the cupboard for you.' She heard purposeful footsteps in the corridor leading to the kitchen and froze.

'Who do you think you are talking to in that tone?' Mr Ranganekar asked pulling her hand away from the tiffin she was fastening shut.

'Leave my hand. I have to deliver these, and I'm already late,' she replied twisting her hand free. She picked up her bag of tiffins and made for the door. Mr Ranganekar grabbed the end of her pallu and yanked it. His wife stumbled but pulled it out from his hand and turned away.

'This can wait,' she told him. 'I have a job to do.' And saying this she unlatched her front door. Mr Ranganekar, enraged, flew at her. Shoving the front door that was closing shut, he caught up to her in the landing outside their flat and roughly turned her around.

'Just who do you think ...' he whispered menacingly, his last words drowned out by the din of falling tiffins. He let her go but it was too late. She stood there as all around her, lids unscrewed and rolled down the stairs, clanging the whole way. Scattered by her feet were wads of notes, slowly being coloured yellow by the spilt daal. Just then the lift doors opened and out stepped the liftman, a mobile phone in his hand.

'Inspector Pandey here, I have the suspect with the goods. Please send the police jeep, I am ready to make an arrest.'

17

Inspector Pandey was home for the first time in months. The night of the arrest, he walked into his apartment and took a deep breath. A servant boy, in frayed shorts and a Superman T-shirt, with the logo almost bleached out from repeated washings, busied himself with turning on the lights and opening doors. After some perfunctory push-ups and a shower, Inspector Pandey shouted for his dinner. Once seated at the table, dressed in a crisp white kurta pyjama, he rolls up his sleeves, and tearing a hot roti with his hands, plunged into his dinner. It had been ages since he last had non-vegetarian food, going undercover as a liftman meant he had to give up on meat and exercise. He was already on his second helping of chicken curry when he slumped back into his chair and thought of

...ast twelve months spent trailing the lead he had gotten on the Ranganekars.

It had been relatively easy to pay off the liftman of Paradise Towers and take his place. The tough part of the job: the mind-numbing hours spent sitting on a wobbly wooden stool in the lift, waiting to carry the residents to and from their respective floors. The last few weeks, with the Singhs moving in and the activity that created, were some respite. He threw himself wholeheartedly into the lifting and shifting of boxes, which was good exercise for his stiff, unused joints. Otherwise it was day after day of sitting and watching, trying to engage the residents in conversation, and during off hours, working on the staff, hoping to win their confidence and get details about their employers and of life within the flats. Nobody really ever suspected anything. The Ranganekars were quiet, and kept to themselves. They hardly every entertained and paid all society dues on time. No one had anything to say about them, and they in turn had nothing to say about anyone. Even when they rode the elevator alone, husband and wife never discussed personal matters or their neighbours.

Interesting, isn't it? Inspector Pandey thought to himself. *How a khaki uniform rendered a liftman invisible, while it made a policeman visible from miles away.* It was unimaginable what people had to say about each other when they don't think they are being heard.

In the course of the year, Inspector Pandey got to know the residents of Paradise Towers well, one could say better than most spouses knew each other. He knew well before Mrs Roy about Mr Roy's diversions to the Patel flat for a snack. That Dinesh skimmed money off all the household purchases – he was saving to buy Lata a pair of gold bangles. He knew Patrick was a drunk and a fool, never a good cocktail. That the Singhs' youngest son was stealing his father's cigarettes, and selling them at school – an entrepreneur or criminal in the making, he thought to himself with a smirk. Inspector Pandey having observed Sam Singh also knew that he was the right boy for Shaana Roy, and it was futile for Mrs Roy to oppose their friendship. The boy was determined. He felt the same way about the Aly Khans, who were asking for trouble with their unnecessary confinement of the beautiful and kind Laila. There was only so much policing a teenager in love was willing to take.

Pandey also suspected Mr Ranganekar beat his wife, his years of police training had equipped him to pick up on the signs. But he had no proof, and he had to choose his battles wisely, no point alerting the Ranganekars by probing into their lives – they were skittish by default. Of all the residents at the Paradise

Towers, who, he had interacted with and formed opinions of at leisure, he found Lata the most exemplary and decent. And though he was inured, courtesy his real job, to the atrocities humans were capable of, the months working undercover at Paradise Towers had convinced him, that he would rather throw in his lot with criminals, who had no delusions of virtue, than befriend the so-called honest citizens of society, who had many a comment on people less fortunate than themselves, whether by dint of birth or circumstance. But in their daily beliefs, prejudices and practices, they were to be feared more than the many unsavoury characters he had, in his long career, put behind bars. Shaking himself out of his reverie, he reached for the remote, and turning on the television, diverted his mind to the vagaries of the world, satisfied that yet another mission had been successful.

The Ranganekars' arrest that morning was followed by two days of heavy rain. The roads became flooded of muddy brown water. Schools were declared shut on account of the flooding and busses being stuck, sometimes for hours on their routes. The women of Paradise Towers, and their children, were forced to stay home, left with not much to do but track the weather on the news or visit each other for tea. Naturally, the Ranganekars dominated all conversation.

Mrs Patel declared she always had a feeling something was just not right about them. 'Mrs Ranganekar used to prepare dabbas, yet not once did she invite us over to have a meal or bring any food for our gatherings. That is when I began to suspect there was something not right about that couple,' she said.

'Why did you not warn us, then? After all, not everyone has your foresight,' replied Mrs Roy, rolling her eyes. Mrs Patel, letting the jibe slide, reached for a plate of kebabs and popping one in her mouth passed them on to the other ladies. They were at Mrs Aly Khan's home again. Outside, the skies were overcast and angry, the trees in the compound swayed so violently that a few lost their branches. Thankfully no one was hurt as the children were usually bundled off to Mrs Singh's flat where they occupied themselves till it was dinnertime and they were called back to their respective homes.

A little pink, plastic bucket stood in the corner, under a leak. Every so often, Mrs Aly Khan would call out for Lata who would emerge – eyes swollen from crying, her head bent – and run to the bucket, which she would empty and replace. Mrs Kapoor, whose gaze did not leave the girl till she disappeared into the kitchen, followed her progress. She was well aware that Dinesh and Lata were no longer talking, and it hurt her pride that Lata should think of throwing her

Dinesh off. She was an impudent, foolish girl who Dinesh had spoilt to the point that she started thinking above her station. She would never find a boy as good as Dinesh. Mrs Kapoor felt the ill effects of this break up very keenly. Dinesh was not his usual resourceful, efficient self. He had become forgetful and sloppy, and needed to be reminded about chores repeatedly. He spent most of his time on a stool in the kitchen looking at his phone, hoping for a call or message from Lata, which never arrived.

'Mrs Ranganekar is a victim of abuse!' said Mrs Roy emphatically. Since the arrest, Shaana Roy had built up the courage to confide in her mother about what she and Sam had seen that day, when she was sent to summon their neighbour.

'I have been to the police station and given my statement. My daughter is an eyewitness. Such women need to be protected and rehabilitated, not thrown in jail,' she continued passionately.

The other ladies nodded in agreement. For a minute, they were all lost in thought. It was sobering, the idea that someone who lived under their roof was being abused and they had never suspected. In fact, they gave the lady a fair amount of flak for never really integrating with the rest of the building. Then their thoughts went to their own marriages, yes, they had complaints with their spouses but those were minor in comparison to what Mrs Ranganekar had been through. Their hearts filled with love and respect for their spouses, whom only a day ago were being vilified as their wives cursed their luck forever meeting and marrying them.

'So what will happen to Mrs Ranganekar now?' asked Mrs Patel.

'Well, she should be let off, she was not a willing participant. She did everything under fear and duress!' replied Mrs Roy. 'If she helps the police by giving them whatever information she has, I hope they let her go.'

Over the course of the two rained-out days, Mrs Kapoor had brought her friends and neighbours up to speed on the nefarious goings on at the Ranganekar home. When Mr Ranganekar had lost his job and subsequently his good nature, he had taken to spending his mornings – while his wife was out at work – at a tea stall in the market near their building. This tea stall was next to a garage that got customers who needed number plates changed overnight or bullet holes covered up in a matter of hours. As they waited for their repairs to get done, the owners of these vehicles would head to the stall for refreshments. Mr Ranganekar fell in with this crowd and soon he began sharing with them the tragic tale of his joblessness. Before he knew it, his new friends had proposed an idea that would make him richer than he could imagine, and with very little risk. All he had to do was collect a briefcase full of notes from them at the tea stall and have the notes secreted into special dabbas, which they would happily supply him with. Surely he married a woman who could cook, they said. All she had to do was distribute the notes amongst the tiffins, stuffing them into a specially designed compartment, and hand it over to the dabbawallah who came to collect it. The dabbawallah was an innocent conduit, the tiffin would be delivered to an accomplice who would then have the money removed and the empty dabbas sent back.

Mr Ranganekar agreed, went home, forced his wife to quit her job, and intimidated her into starting this new one. When she begged him to allow better sense to prevail, better they be poor than go against the law, she was beaten till she was unable to speak. In this way, the Ranganekars became complicit in one of the most notorious fake currency rings in the country. They eventually became richer than Mr Ranganekar could have ever imagined. They bought themselves a flat in the fancy building – Paradise Towers – in their neighbourhood, set themselves up with the best amenities money could buy and began to live a lifestyle they never imagined within their grasp. Mr Ranganekar told his neighbours he worked for a newspaper, and every morning he left with his briefcase for work. But instead he spent his day whiling away time at the tea stall, sometimes going for a walk on the beach with his newfound friends or catching the matinee show of a much-anticipated movie.

Mrs Ranganekar's life grew bleaker; she was denied basic freedom of expression and was increasingly shut off from the rest of the world. A fortnightly visit to her parents was all the human interaction she had. Her husband forbade her to fraternize with the neighbours and she reconciled to staring out the peephole at whatever activity livened up the building. She grew sullen and spent most of her time in prayer. Her marriage deteriorated; her husband barely tolerated her and she loathed him. Many a night she thought of killing herself but by morning she changed her mind, lacking the courage. Every time her spouse beat her, he would return the next day with a gift, in an attempt to make amends – a silk sari, gold, new shoes, tickets to a movie, dinner at a fancy restaurant. At first, she refused to accept them, but that would cost her. Once her husband flew into such a rage when she refused to accept gold coins that he shoved them into her mouth till she almost choked on them. After that, she decided it was simpler to take them, but she never wore anything he gave her, unless he specifically asked her to. And so things had continued for them until the day of their arrest.

By the time Mrs Kapoor had finished recounting her story, Mrs Patel, tears streaming down her face, her nose read from repeated blowing of it into a napkin, had finished the entire plate of kebabs and had started on the pakoras. Mrs Singh, thinking that if she did not stop her friend she would be in danger of doing herself serious harm, moved the plate off the table and handed it to Lata, who took it back to the kitchen with her as Mrs Patel's eyes longingly followed them in. Mrs Roy was indignant, and in this mood, had let slip a couple of stitches from her crocheting, which angered her even further. Frustrated, she unravelled the whole thing and shoved it back into her knitting basket. Mrs Aly Khan and Singh sat stunned, their hands over gaping mouths. And Mrs Kapoor, her job done, folded the napkin on her lap into a tiny square and sat back on her sofa. She pulled out her mobile phone from her handbag and saw that she had no less than five missed calls from her mother.

On hearing of the arrest made in her daughters building, which was now national news, the headlines screaming out the name of Paradise Towers, painting it to be a veritable den of vice, it was impossible that Mrs Kapoor's mother not be kept abreast of developments. However, with so much happening in the building, Mrs Kapoor did not have the time to indulge her mother …

so she put the phone back into her bag and zipped it shut, turning her full attention to her friends.

Meanwhile, Laila Aly Khan lay on her bed, her toes playing with the curtain. For the past few weeks she had been crying herself to sleep and waking up with migraines. Even the slightest sliver of sunlight would get her head pounding again so she took to sitting with the curtains drawn all day. Aroon would be in class right now, she thought to herself. He would call her when he was done. They had been in touch every day since her mother confronted her, but they were still unable to come up with a solution. To think that Laila's misery would dull her beauty would be to not appreciate it enough, for right now as she lay heartbroken and depleted from crying, she looked even more ravishing.

It broke Lata's heart that her charge be withering away like this. Laila had to be forced to eat her meals and many a time, Lata would have to spoon-feed her. It was a task with the young girl pushing her hand away and only relenting when Lata reasoned that Aroon would want his old Laila back once all this was done. Lata was sick with guilt, what Dinesh had done was unforgiveable, she had refused to meet him alone, averting her head if he came into view in the public areas of the building. There was a code of honour and he had broken it, she wanted to have nothing to do with him anymore.

Outside, the chatter of the women grew more animated and Laila put in her earphones and turned up her music, falling back onto her pillow, waving her hand at Lata to leave the room. Lata walked to the door and stifled a sob as she saw Laila pull out her phone and flip through pictures of Aroon and her in happier times, as tears welled up yet again in her eyes.

18

A piercing screech ripped through the early morning air. It was followed by the amplification of a thumping sound that managed to wake up even the most reluctant of risers. Mr Singh being one such person. With eyes still shut, he reached out to his nightstand, his fingers searching for a pair of earplugs. His blind fiddling not only managed to dislodge the earplugs, sending them rolling off the stand and under the bed where they would disappear, but also his mobile phone. This immediately woke him up and throwing his cover aside, he got out of bed, rubbed his hands over his face and retrieved his phone. He then put on his slippers and walked into the living room.

His wife was seated on the balcony reading the papers, a mug of steaming coffee on the table beside her. Mr Singh walked up to her and kissing her on the top of her head, picked up her mug and took a gulp. 'Have you brushed your teeth?' his wife asked tilting her head up and looking at him, squinting against the sunlight. To this, Mr Singh shook his head. She grabbed her mug back from his hands and ordered him to go wash up. 'What's all this noise?' Mr Singh asked pointing to the garden of the building that their balcony looked over. 'Diwali tomorrow, or have you forgotten? Our first in India, the building has a party of sorts every year. The kids are excited and participating,' she replied, folding her paper onto itself and standing up.

'This building has way too many get-togethers, darling,' Mr Singh said, rubbing his eyes before turning to walk back into his bedroom, when a thought occurred to him and he slowly turned back to his wife and asked, 'That was our son doing a mic test, wasn't it? What is he doing now? Singing? Dancing? … I don't know why you encourage this nonsense,' – he was building up to an agitated rant when his wife stopped him. 'He is DJing, that's all. Don't give him grief for it.'

Relieved Mr Singh walked away and Mrs Singh, shaking her head from side to side, called out to the cook to prepare her husband's breakfast.

Across the floor, Mr Roy dropped breadcrumbs all over his shirt as he bit into his toast, his entire focus on a book about the British Empire. His tea, largely neglected, had formed a thin film of wrinkled skin, and was getting cold. From the top of his book he watched Mrs Roy busying herself in the kitchen. She was making traditional Diwali sweets for the building party and had paid scant attention to anything else that morning. Seeing that she was well distracted, he opened his satchel and pulled out a round, steel-lidded box and opened it. Mrs Patel had very generously sent across some freshly made poha for him, and he inhaled the aroma, his mouth watering. Surreptitiously he spooned some out onto his plate and began shovelling it into his mouth, scalding his tongue. He heard giggling and was alerted to his daughter, Shaana and their neighbour's son, Sam sitting on the other end of the table. The children dropped their heads when he looked at them and pretended to busy themselves with stringing fresh marigold as part of the décor for the next day's party. Mr Roy cleared his throat and the youngsters looked up at him, smiling at his fogged-up spectacles. He pushed the box towards them and silently gestures for them to help themselves. Sam served Shaana a large spoonful before helping himself. He closed the lid and slid it back to Mr Roy, who quickly hid it back in his satchel. They all shared a conspiratorial look and tucked in, smacking their lips after. It was delicious indeed.

The Patel house was in disarray. All the children had been sent downstairs to help with the setting up. Mrs Patel and her staff had turned the kitchen into an assembly line from which emerged all kinds of edibles. Mithai and trays of dry fruit were kept, for want of space, on the sofas. A line of ladies, Lata amongst them, were sitting cross-legged on the floor, shaping little samosa parcels, which would be fried the next day in time for the party. Oblivious to all this, Mr Patel sat on the only chair not occupied by trays of food, and was focused on the flickering ticker tape of share prices rising and falling on the television. Every so often, his wife put a plate of something to nibble on in front of him and he, without even looking at it, put it in his mouth.

The doorbell rang at the Aly Khan flat and the door was opened to let in the cook and an assistant, laden with industrial-sized dishes, on loan – both cook and dishes – to Mrs Aly Khan from her mother-in-law. The Aly Khan children were busy stringing fairy lights on the bushes bordering the garden. Twice already Laila had been sent down to tend to a splinter and untangle one of her siblings from the lights. The Patel girls were placing little mud diyas on round tables and arranging the chairs. Mrs Singh's sons were helping their brother wire and set up the DJ booth in one corner, occasionally whispering 'testing 1...2...3 we can see Sam's undies for free' into the mic, their courage doubled because Sam was not present to hear this.

By mid-afternoon, most of the arrangements were done and the children took to running around the tables or grouping together, chatting and laughing. The gardener was watering the plants for the second time that day when Mrs Kapoor walked in, both hands full with heavy cloth bags. She lumbered her way to the lift then put them down, calling for the elevator. She spotted her kids in the garden from the corner of her eye and bellowed out to them. They reluctantly left their friends and walked to their mother, dragging their feet and stuffing their phones into their pockets. Mrs Kapoor took one look at their dirty hands and faces, with little black smudges on the nose and mouth, and instructed them to get into the elevator with her, handing them some of her load. Stopping to get off at Mrs Singh's flat, she rang the doorbell, her children carrying on to their own home where they had been asked to wash their faces. Mrs Singh opened her front door and beckoned her neighbour come in. Mrs Kapoor, declining the offer, stood in the foyer, giving Mrs Singh the time for later that day, to assemble at the lobby so they could start their rangoli there before working their way up floor by floor.

Mrs Singh confirmed she would be there when Mrs Kapoor spotted Mr Singh sitting in the living room, watching TV. She had very little interaction with the man and decided it was a good time to befriend him, and suddenly agreed to come in for a bit and have a cup of tea with the Singhs before heading back up. Mr Singh, now stuck between his wife and their neighbour, worked himself up into a sour mood. Having luxuriated the entire morning in a home devoid of boys running around, or having to break up fights, he had finally settled after lunch to watch a baseball match he had downloaded. A beer in his hand he was getting well into the swing of things when he was rudely interrupted and now sat here having to make small talk. Mrs Singh suggested they take their tea out to the balcony, it being a beautiful day. Down in the garden her sons had got their equipment set and were testing out some music. The atmosphere was building up and she was beginning to look forward to the Diwali party. They settled into their seats, after a round of changing places so Mrs Kapoor would not have the sun on her face, and sipped their drinks.

Mr Singh looked at his watch for the fifth time and got a dirty look from his wife for doing so, when a rickshaw pulled up in front of the gate. From it came Mrs Ranganekar. She walked in through the open side gate, and towards the building. Mrs Kapoor froze, forgetting her tea and her chance to fraternize with her neighbours that would only add to her cache of information. She made an excuse about needing to head home so as not to leave the children alone with her husband, who would not appreciate the disturbance on his day off. Apologizing for the trouble she put them through for the tea, she hastily left their apartment. Running down one floor to the lobby she soon found herself face to face with Mrs Ranganekar. The first thing that struck Mrs Kapoor about her neighbour was that she had gained some weight and that it suited her very well. Prison food must suit her, she thought and without any hesitation reached out and enveloped Mrs Ranganekar in a tight hug. Mrs Ranganekar started, she was never comfortable with physical affection and her years of abuse had made her skittish and wary when touched. 'Mrs Ranganekar, when were you released from prison? We've all been following your case carefully but never read about it in the papers. I would like you to know on behalf of all at Paradise Towers, all our sympathies are with you,' Mrs Kapoor rattled off without even pausing to breathe.

'Thank you, Mrs Kapoor,' the hapless lady replied, struggling free of the hug. 'I was let off without any charge days after the arrest,' she said.

'Oh! I see,' said Mrs Kapoor, astonished more at her lack of knowledge than the lady's acquittal.

'Yes. I chose to go live with my parents and have been there these past weeks.'

'Oh, yes I completely understand. Nothing like your mother's home when times are bad,' Mrs Kapoor said thinking wistfully of her own mother for a moment.

'After everything that happened I did not have the spirit to come back to my flat, Mrs Kapoor. I am in fact, here to empty it, I would like to put it on the market.'

Before Mrs Kapoor could say anything, the lift that had been called by Mrs Ranganekar came to a stop at the lobby and Mrs Roy emerged from it. Surprised to see her, it took her a minute before Mrs Roy could find the words to speak. Lacking Mrs Kapoor's ebullience she reached out and took Mrs Ranganekar's hand, and the other woman responded with a smile. This silent interlude was broken up by Mrs Kapoor declaring, 'Mrs Ranganekar is here to put her flat up for sale, Mrs Roy.'

'Oh!' said Mrs Roy. 'That is unfortunate, could we not persuade you to stay on?' Mrs Ranganekar was taken aback, she did not expect her neighbours to want to have anything to do with her after the arrest and imprisonment of her husband and herself. 'I ... I did not think we would be welcome back here, Mrs Roy,' she said.

'Well, I do not think there is any chance of Mr Ranganekar being let out of jail any time soon, he would definitely not be welcome here but you, Mrs Ranganekar, you should not have to leave your home,' replied Mrs Roy emphatically. Not to be outdone by Mrs Roy, Mrs Kapoor also chimed in: 'Yes, you are always welcome. Better the devil you know, isn't it? Who knows what kind of person will buy your flat and we will be stuck with a stranger,' she said in an unfortunately worded plea.

'I would have to give it some thought,' said a shaken Mrs Ranganekar before excusing herself and entering the lift, which carried her up to her flat. Mrs Kapoor was left smiling to herself for being fortuitous enough to waylay the lady thus getting first dibs on all the news. Mrs Roy looked disapprovingly at her neighbour, knowing all too well what was going through the lady's brain.

19

The news of Mrs Ranganekar's return spread all over the building like wildfire, not least because of Mrs Kapoor's valiant efforts to ensure it. By the next morning, every single one of her neighbours had paid a visit to Mrs Ranganekar, assuring her of their support, and assistance if she so required it, and their willingness for her to stay on at Paradise Towers and reconsider the selling of her flat.

After a restless night, conflicted between the violent and unpleasant memories the place brought up and the overwhelming kindness of her neighbours, Mrs Ranganekar woke up on Diwali morning with her mind made up. She had decided to stay on, leaving meant accepting defeat and she was not going to let that happen. After a long and arduous phone call with her parents, where she finally managed to convince them of her decision, she set about cleaning up her reclaimed home, and stepped out to do some household shopping. On the way out, having taken the stairs, she walked past the Singhs' flat. Their door was open and Mrs Singh was handing the dhobi and his wife an envelope that would contain their Diwali bakshish. Mrs Ranganekar waved to her neighbour and wished her a happy Diwali. Mrs Singh reciprocated and invited the lady in for some hot coffee she had just brewed. Mrs Ranganekar declined, she had to get her flat back into shape if she wanted to have things up and running so she could attend the party later that night. She thanked Mrs Singh and said she would meet her later in the evening. As she left the building, the watchman fashioned her a salute and she smiled back at him. It was a beautiful day. The sun was out and the garden was in full bloom, embellished with tables and chairs for the night's festivities. For the first time in years Mrs Ranganekar felt light, there was a spring in her step. She was happy.

The remainder of the day had the residents of Paradise Towers occupied in organizing their homes. Those who observed Laxmi pooja busied themselves with setting up their mandirs for it, decorating the idols with flowers and lighting diyas. Gifts of new clothes and money were exchanged within the family and staff were given a bonus and packets of sweets. Everyone was in a festive mood. The younger occupants of Paradise Towers were restless, eager for the party to start. In the early evening, they visited each other with gifts of mithai and dry fruit, and then retired to their own homes to change into their Diwali finery and begin their poojas.

Mrs Ranganekar stood in her flat, swept clean of all the debris from months of disuse. A cool wind blew in through the open windows and ran through the house. She breathed in the sweet smells of ghee from the diyas that were being lit all over the building. Her doorbell rang, and wondering who it could be, she went to answer it. On the other side stood Mrs Aly Khan, Laila, her daughter, and Lata, their maid.

'Mrs Ranganekar, happy Diwali,' said Mrs Aly Khan as Mrs Ranganekar invited them in. 'I have brought you some of our homemade gaajar halwa,' she said as Laila handed her a glass bowl from which emanated the most heavenly aroma. Mrs Rangakenar coloured. 'Thank you, I am afraid I have nothing to give you. I am just about getting my bearings together,' she replied, taking the bowl from Laila and keeping it on the counter top in her kitchen as the guests made their way into the living room. Against a wall, Mrs Ranganekar had set up and decorated her mandir, and it was aglow with marigold and diyas.

'Perhaps we have disturbed you in the middle of your pooja?' asked Mrs Aly Khan.

'No, not at all. I haven't even started yet,' Mrs Ranganekar replied before asking if she could get her guests something to drink, which they declined.

'If it is alright with you, could we sit with you while you do your pooja?' asked Laila shyly. Mrs Ranganekar, her eyes brimming with tears, smiled and holding the girl by her hand showed them to the mandir, where they all sat cross legged on the floor. Mrs Ranganekar went about her ritual cleaning of the idols before decorating them with flowers and vermillion. Offering the deities fruits and mithai, she requested Lata to bring some of the halwa from the kitchen and that too she offered to her gods before starting her prayers. As she sat singing the arti, Mrs Ranganekar's heart was bursting with gratitude. This was indeed a new beginning. Tomorrow, she thought, she would look into getting her old job back. The pooja ended and the ladies sat eating halwa, which Lata had quickly warmed up on the stove.

'Let's have a cup of tea before we head down to the party,' suggested Mrs Aly Khan. 'That way we give Mrs Patel time to organize her food...' she said, and everyone laughed as Lata put tea leaves and milk to boil.

As night fell, the garden lit up as hundreds of little lights came to life. Hanging from the trees were white paper lanterns gently swaying in the wind. Round tables were scattered around the garden and by and by people occupied them. At the far end, Mrs Singh's son was fiddling with buttons and knobs before starting his music. Next to the makeshift DJ booth, which was an iPad connected to some speakers, was a dance floor: a few slats of wood painted by the children in multi coloured stars and rainbows.

Standing on it, gazing at the DJ with awe, were the younger Aly Khan and Kapoor boys. Shaana Roy walked in with her parents, she was in a red chiffon sari that had a gold border. Her hair was dried and smoothened off of all its curls, and it fell to her waist shining like silk. She had worn gold earrings that dangled as she walked, and had forgone wearing her glasses so she could line her eyes with kaajal. On her feet she had on paayals and though she walked with a slight limp, her leg having not regained its complete strength after her cast was removed, she looked regal. She held on to her father's hand as he steered her to one of the tables. Sam Singh, captivated by Shaana in all her glory, sat staring at her till a sharp elbow to the rib by one of the Patel girls snapped him out of it. He got up and went to the Roys, wishing them and then turning to Shaana wished her too and asked her if she would like to join him at the other table. Mrs Roy knew exactly what Sam felt for her daughter.

and not approving of him at all, put her hand on her daughter's arm to keep her from going. But before she could say anything, Mr Roy slapped the boy on the back and said, 'Run along Shaana, go sit with your friends. What will you do here with us oldies.'

Shaana, kissing her father on the cheek, got up to go. Mrs Roy shot her husband a dirty look and grimaced, saying, ' You don't encourage this boy now, he is a no-gooder, always being suspended from school. Is this the influence you want for our daughter?'

'He is a good boy. Shaana has opened up so much in his company. It is good she makes friends. These are their years to get into trouble. Let her enjoy them,' her husband answered, placating her by putting his arm around her in a hug. Shaana took a few uneven steps before turning to Sam. She whispered in his ear, 'Sam, without my glasses I'm almost blind, I don't know where I'm going.' Sam Singh, breaking out in goosebumps from her breath in his ear, reached out for her hand and entwining her fingers in his, walked her to his table. Seeing this, Mrs Roy turned red in indignation and pointing it out to her husband said, 'Shameless boy, he is holding her hand like this in front of everyone. This is not America!'

Mr Roy, calming her down, said, 'Don't you remember when we would hold hands and walk? Come, let me take you for a dance, for old times' sake.' Mrs Roy blushed, flattered at the attention her husband was lavishing on her and they walked to the dance floor, hand in hand.

Mrs Patel's silk blouse was wet with perspiration. She had arranged then re-arranged the serving dishes of food three times already, swapping the rice to first one end of the line-up and then the other. She gave instructions to the staff, borrowed from all her neighbours' homes, on how to keep the food warm, and reminded them to not forget to serve everyone her Gujrati kadi – it was a speciality. Mr and Mrs Singh joined the Roys on the dance floor and the party was in full swing when Mrs Aly Khan, Laila and Mrs Ranganekar arrived with Lata following just behind them.

As Lata made her way to the buffet tables, Dinesh caught up with her, and keeping pace with her as she quickened her speed, tried to strike up a conversation: 'Lata, wait... happy Diwali.' Lata refused to answer and instead greeted her friends from among the staff that worked in the other flats. 'Lata, I had to say something to protect you, my madam had noticed we were spending a lot of time together. I did not want her thinking you were loose,' he explained. Lata turned around to face Dinesh, her eyes furious. 'Never speak to me again, what you did is unforgiveable. I can protect myself, I do not need you to do that and I do not care what your madam thinks of my character. She is the biggest gossip in this building and everyone is afraid to share anything with her,' Lata shot back venomously. 'Poor Mrs Aly Khan, to have a friend like that ... I pity her but they are big people and who am I to warn her? For weeks I have seen Laila baby cry herself to sleep, hardly eat, withering away before my eyes. Even her education has been stopped. I wish I had never met you, Dinesh. Someone who is willing to harm another to protect themselves can never be a friend of mine.' And it dawned on Dinesh that he had lost her forever. Lata would never speak to him again. His heart sank and he stood rooted to the ground as she walked away from him.

Mrs Kapoor, spotting Mrs Ranganekar, waved out frantically to her and gestured her join her table. The ladies walked over and finding seats next to Mrs Kapoor, readied themselves for the barrage of questions that would follow.

Mrs Patel walked towards the Roys, who had taken a breather from the dancing and were having their dinner in companionable silence. Spotting her coming towards them, Mr Roy began to get anxious. What if she asked him about the poha? His wife would be furious. He started to sweat profusely, wiping his brow with a handkerchief. 'Mrs Roy!' called Mrs Patel, and Mrs Roy turned to face her. 'Mrs Roy! Never in my life have I tasted such mithai. Mr Patel had to get me away from the buffet table ... see I have taken.' Opening up a paper napkin that had three pieces of sandesh, she waved it under her own nose, closing her eyes in delight. 'You have to promise me, Mrs Roy, whenever you make sandesh, do not forget your neighbours across the corridor.' She then pulled up a chair and sat down, popping another mithai in her mouth.

Mrs Roy, wiping her mouth with the end of her napkin, smiled. 'Of course, Mrs Patel, of course! You tell me any time you want them I will make them especially for you! Happy Diwali, Mrs Patel.' She embraced her one-time foe.

'Mr Roy, how did you...' carried on Mrs Patel between mouthfuls when her husband appeared behind her, and sensing trouble, asked her to come help him with his dinner by the buffet table. Mrs Patel, struggling to gather her napkin of food, rushed off, regaling her husband with high praise for the exquisite sandesh. As she left the table, Mr Roy gave his wife a sheepish smile and went back to eating his dinner.

The night wore on and the residents of Paradise Towers, a tough few months behind them, gave themselves up to the celebrations. Mr Singh performed a vigorous bhangra, his sons secretly filming him as they laughed themselves silly. Even the youngsters got onto the dance floor, moving energetically. The Aly Khans, linking hands with their kids, formed a circle and were dancing away when Mrs Aly Khan noticed Laila's absence. She asked one of her girls to go look for their older sister.

Mrs Aly Khan had begun to believe her eldest daughter was finally over her trauma, and went back to her dancing. That was when Mr Aly Khan felt a tap on his back, stopped dancing and turned to face his second eldest, a note in hand. He opened the note and walked off the dance floor while reading it, his wife noticing this followed him, asking him what happened. After reading the note, Mr Aly Khan quietly handed it to his wife and sat down on a chair, looking at her before saying, 'Can someone explain to me what is going on?'

Mrs Aly Khan started reading, her breath coming faster and heavier as she did, the colour draining from her face. The note was from Laila, and it read:

It pains me to give you grief. I love you both so much, but I also love Aroon and I cannot get him out of my heart. Believe me, I have tried. For weeks I have struggled with what I should do, and finally I have decided that I need to follow my heart. I hope you can understand why I am doing this, and if you cannot I pray that in time you will come to forgive me.

Your Laila

'She has run away! Our Laila has left us and run away,' screamed Mrs Aly Khan before falling to the ground and fainting. As the music came to a sudden stop, everyone rushed towards the Aly Khans. Mrs Kapoor started asking people to clear the way so she could reach her friend.

20

The Aly Khans' flat was full of people. Lata was showing around a tray of water to the worried faces. Inside the bedroom, Mrs Aly Khan was propped up by pillows and a doctor was taking her blood pressure. She kept up a constant moaning. Mr Aly Khan was on the phone with the police and they were sending someone over to take a statement. He ran his hands through his hair and paced the room. Finally, his wife came to with the help of some powerful smelling salts that Mrs Ranganekar had at her flat, and which she used to wake her husband up from a stupor. Mrs Aly Khan told her husband about Laila and Aroon, how she found out, and its consequences that had led to Laila taking this drastic step. Berating herself, she cried out sometimes in anger at her child and sometimes with fear for her daughter's well-being.

'How could you have kept her from college?' Mr Aly Khan chided his wife. 'This is the twenty-first century, there are ways of managing things. We could have met the boy and judged for ourselves. You forced her hand!' he continued, as Mrs Aly Khan broke into fresh wails.

Mr Aly Khan went and sat beside his wife and held her hand. 'I only hope she is safe,' he said with worry creasing his forehead.

Outside, Mr Kapoor had taken his wife aside and stood berating her. 'You are responsible for this, you and your meddling ways have caused such harm and distress to this family. That poor young girl, to think how desperate her state would have had to be to do something like this.'

Mrs Kapoor tried to interject, but she was interrupted by her husband. 'How can you even suggest to Mrs Aly Khan that she not take her husband into confidence? Enough of your meddling. My head hangs in shame and you are responsible for it, perhaps if you did something more constructive with your time than gossip with you mother, this situation would have been averted.' Mrs Kapoor looked up sharply at her husband and gauging from his face that he was in no mood to tolerate any back chat, settled down again, keeping mum.

Mrs Ranganekar stood up and suggested they give the Aly Khans their privacy, and then turning to Mrs Kapoor, said, 'Why don't we take all the children down, surely they should not have to witness this? Let them enjoy their party.' Mrs Kapoor, thankful to have been given a purpose immediately, set to rounding up the children and ushering them downstairs and back into the garden, where within minutes they forgot about the crisis and got to playing amongst themselves again.

Shaana turned to Sam, who was loading her plate with some food from the buffet. 'Poor Laila, imagine none of us knew she was kept home from college.'

'Yeah, that's intense. Like a Hindi movie,' replied Sam, taking Shaana back to the table. They sat down and began eating, Shaana pushing food around her plate because she was unable to make out what was what. The other kids were busy in the distance, dancing on the stage. The music, though at a far lower volume, was still being expertly managed by the young DJ. The lights of the lanterns on the tree they were sitting under flickered and then went off. Sam gave a short laugh 'That's all we needed. Is there always so much drama in this building?' he asked Shaana, who was struggling to find a napkin to wipe her mouth with. Sam, reaching out for the napkin, gently wiped Shaana's mouth. 'Are you really that blind right now? Can't you see anything?' Shaana shook her head. 'So you have no idea how beautiful you look tonight, Shaana?' Sam said, his voice dropping to a gentle whisper. Shaana blushed and shook her head again, barely able to conceal a shy smile.

'Shaana…'

'Yes?'

'I'm going to kiss you,' Sam said, holding her face in his hands. She closed her eyes as his lips touched hers. The lights from the rest of the lanterns flickered as the two lost themselves in their first kiss.

There was a knock on the door and Lata walked into the Aly Khans' bedroom. Mrs Aly Khan had been given a sleeping tablet and was fast asleep. Mr Aly Khan was flicking through channels impatiently, the cordless phone in his hand. 'Sir,' said Lata, her voice barely audible.

'Yes, Lata, what is it?'

'Sir, I have the number for Laila baby's friend,' she said, fear in her voice.

'What? Why didn't you say so earlier? Give it to me,' Mr Aly Khan said, and on being given the number, punched it into the phone and waited.

'Hello?' an adult male voice answered and Mr Aly Khan stood up.

'Hello, this is Mr Aly Khan. Am I speaking with Aroon?'

'Mr Aly Khan, hello. This is Aroon's father,' the voice replied. 'If you are wondering where your daughter is and if she is safe, let me assure you she is. In fact, she is standing here right in front of me,' the voice of Mr Sanghvi explained calmly.

'Thank God,' exclaimed Mr Aly Khan.

'Mr Aly Khan, perhaps this should be something your daughter tells you herself, but I doubt she will be able to. It seems my son and your daughter have just got married. My wife and I had no idea until Aroon walked into our house not ten minutes ago and gave us the news,' a hint of anger coloured his voice as he said this.

'Oh, dear God!' said Mr Aly Khan.

'It seems there was a civil marriage at a common friend's house. I am holding the certificate,' continued Mr Sanghvi.

'Laila, what have you done!' cried Mr Aly Khan, disconnecting the phone and breaking into sobs.

Epilogue

In the year after that fateful Diwali night, the residents of Paradise Towers ambled their way to a more sanguine state of mind.

Mrs Ranganekar got her job back and six months into it, a promotion that finally spurred her on to file for a divorce from Mr Ranganekar, who is still in jail. She soon became the most beloved resident at Paradise Towers, frequently being invited over to one home or the other for dinner, and she seldom ate her meals alone.

Mrs Kapoor, though still addicted to her gossip magazines, took on the mantel from Mrs Ranganekar and used her talents to cook for the dabbawallahs. She waylaid them every time they came for a pick up, and they regaled her with gossip gleaned from their huge network.

Mrs Singh remained busy managing her four boys. Her third son was recording a music video, which he planned to release on YouTube to close to 2,000 followers – something Mrs Singh has not gotten round to telling her husband.

Mrs Patel and Mrs Roy became fast friends, frequently visiting each other at home. Mrs Roy took Mrs Patel under her wing and introduced her to the wonders of Bengali cinema. Mrs Patel, unable to shed her weight joined a gym in the neighbourhood but always surrendered to the cookies in its cafeteria on her way out.

Mr Roy has encouraged the friendship between his wife and neighbour, and reaped the benefits of Mrs Patel's culinary skills.

Shaana and Sam celebrated their one-year anniversary, still just as besotted with each other – much to Mrs Roy's annoyance. Under Shaana's influence, Sam Singh managed to pass just about all his exams and Mrs Singh finally found in her the daughter she never had. Shaana also invested in contact lenses.

The Aly Khans had a rough year. Mrs Aly Khan was ostracized by her in-laws and no longer visited their home for their weekly lunch. She had lunch with her friends at home instead, which she infinitely preferred.

Her relationship with Mrs Kapoor, though strained, remained polite. They seldom spoke on the phone.

Mrs Aly Khan refused to have anything to do with her daughter or son-in-law. Mr Aly Khan, though, would call Laila on his way to work – unbeknownst to his wife.

Lata, after admitting to the Aly Khans that she was responsible for procuring a phone for Laila so she could communicate with Aroon, was in danger of losing her job. After much begging and pleading she was kept on, but lost all contact with Laila and refused to speak with Dinesh.

Laila and Aroon Sanghvi enjoyed their blissful happiness together. Laila, being a good-natured girl, took to her in-laws and they to her. She went back to college and after completing her course, began helping out her mother-in-law with her design label, which made evening clutches.

Aroon joined the family business, doing well. His father had decided to send Laila and him abroad to handle their international branch.

By the time Laila and Aroon visited her family at Paradise Towers for the first time in a year, Mrs Aly Khan had finally reconciled to their relationship, thanks to Mr Aly Khan, who convinced her to see their daughter before her imminent departure.

Mrs Mody's flat, which had remained empty, was to finally get an occupant. A moving van waited outside the gate as movers walked in and out bringing things to the third-floor flat. The ladies of Paradise Towers gathered at Mrs Singh's for a coffee and waited anxiously on the balcony, trying to spot their new neighbour. They kept fanning themselves with the *Hello* magazines that lay scattered on the table in front of them.

Mrs Singh complimented Mrs Roy on her wonderful daughter, but Mrs Roy did not reciprocate with one for Sam. A red sports car pulled up and honked at the watchman who ran to open the gate, adjusting his cap while trying to peek in through the tinted windows. A chauffeur in white uniform got off and opened the back door. There was a collective gasp on Mrs Singh's balcony and Mrs Kapoor – hyperventilating in excitement – opened the magazine, quickly turning the pages before stabbing her finger repeatedly on a picture. Everyone turned to look at the picture and then the person who had just walked out of the car and was instructing the mover. And just like that, Paradise Towers had its new tenant.

Acknowledgements

There are a few people without whom this book would not have been possible, and whom I would like to thank.

Nikhil, who first read a few scribbled pages of *Paradise Towers* and saw potential in it.

Sarita Tanwar, my first de facto boss, who opened the door to the world and pushed me to step outside.

Kaajal Anand, who has been a rock, cheerleader, trouble-shooter, advisor and a solid friend.

Rinke Khanna, for her support and faith, and amazing proof-reading skills. And for her weekly book recommendations – I love you.

Anuj Bahri and Aanchal Malhotra, who took a chance on a bookworm and got her publish-worthy – you guys are the best.

Anu Dewaan, for graciously opening her Alibaug home to me so that I could meet my deadline – thank you, without you I wouldn't have been able to complete *Paradise Towers*.

Shreya Punj, for making me comfortable and showing such enthusiasm in my work and having my back. Diya, Shabnam and Akriti – thank you for being the best team a girl could ask for.

Benu, for all her love and nurturing and introducing me to the term 'Bizzy Lizzy'.

Last but not the least – my children, Navya and Agastya, for just being who they are. You make my job so easy. And for allowing me my creative space. You are invaluable. My parents, for always being the wind beneath my wings. And Abhishek, my brother, for being my anchor.